SONG OF CORPUS JURIS

By Joe L. Hensley

SONG OF CORPUS JURIS
THE POISON SUMMER
LEGISLATIVE BODY
DELIVER US TO EVIL
THE COLOR OF HATE

SONG OF CORPUS JURIS

JOE L. HENSLEY

PUBLISHED FOR THE CRIME CLUB BY
DOUBLEDAY & COMPANY, INC.
GARDEN CITY, NEW YORK
1974

All of the characters in this book are fictitious, and any resemblance to actual persons, living or dead, is purely coincidental.

Library of Congress Cataloging in Publication Data

Hensley, Joe L 1926–
Song of corpus juris.
I. Title.
PZ4.H525So [PS3558.E55] 813'.5'4
ISBN 0-385-09555-4
Library of Congress Catalog Card Number 74-3694

Copyright © 1974 by Joe L. Hensley
All Rights Reserved
Printed in the United States of America
First Edition

For Harlan, Friend

SONG OF
CORPUS JURIS

Circuit Judge Harold Steinmetz nodded his courteous aging head once more. We had been doing bitter battle on a petition to let to bail for three days now and mercifully we were about done. Steinmetz looked tiredly around his musty courtroom where the framed pictures of his predecessors on the bench stared back at him.

"Ah," he said. "Do either of you two gentlemen have anything further to add before I make my decision?" He stared at me and I had a premonition about his decision that was bad for me, worse for Mary Ann Moffat.

Frank Lucas bobbed to his feet. He's younger than I am, quick and energetic. He's deputy prosecutor and works therefore for Herman Leaks, which is a disability, but we drink coffee now and then and insult each other carefully and mostly get along well. But just now he was enduring his first taste of political heat and trying to do his valiant best for his boss Herman Leaks, the prosecutor, trying for Herman not to mess it up with the important man who sat beside him frowning and lovingly stroking the tiny scars I'd noticed where his hair began to thin behind his ears, a nervous habit.

Leaks himself had been in and out of court a dozen times while the score of witnesses had testified, watching it all and keeping a watchful hand on the switches. Yet he'd taken no active part, perhaps because he knew that I had knowledge that he'd once dated my client's mother.

"May it please the court," Lucas said. "The state strongly urges that bond for Mary Ann Moffat be denied. We contend that the proof has been evident, nay overwhelming, that she committed the crime of first degree murder. We have presented three eyewitnesses to the shooting death of Roger Tuttle, we've introduced evidence concerning the weapon and how many shots were fired from it, and we've shown where the defendant acquired it. It's true that we've not shown that the defendant harbored any malice toward the deceased victim, Roger Tuttle, but we have shown she was resentful and angry with her former stepfather, Joseph Watts." He nodded at the man sitting next to him. Watts sat stiffly, not looking back, enduring it all. He was very handsome, but he was along in years a bit. I'd never met the man socially, but I knew about him, a lot about him. Any citizen of Bington, my town, who could read or who frequented a barber shop, which might run up as high as seventy per cent of the male population, knew about him. He was a man of power even in this off year. He was the current state chairman of that *other* party. He was constantly being mentioned by them as a possible candidate for elective offices up to and including governor. I'd heard it said around that he didn't much like me and that he'd announced same publicly a few times. I'd beaten one of his own for the area legislative seat once. He'd personally declared that they'd get that seat back from me and they had. In Bington the job hadn't been too hard. I was now an ex-legislator, happy and without bitterness.

Watts was in his fifties and the gossipers I'd heard said he had enough money to buy what he couldn't get as a favor by political intrigue. He had suspiciously black hair, luxuriant as a lawn in spring, a trim body which showed the effect of a health spa somewhere, and wore a suit I'd decided cost a lot of money. He'd been accompanied into the courtroom on this day by two other gentlemen who now awaited him beyond the rail. They sat in the midst of a cluster of news media people and other hangers-on. I knew Watts's two friends pretty well. One of them was the local county chairman for Watts's party, a man named Suedell, Alvin Suedell. He'd given me a grin once and a secret wink. The other was a man I'd known as a boy, grown up with. His name was Ted Polly. Both worked for/with Watts. Both had testified as eyewitnesses to the killing of Roger Tuttle along with their compatriot Watts and various police officers, lab technicians, hospital personnel, etc.

Frank Lucas hammered on: "The defense, on the other hand, called no witnesses to counteract our case in chief. The defense has been merely content to find the extent of our case and to enter a smattering of questionable temporary insanity evidence." He looked over at me with some heat in his eyes and I smiled at him.

He said: "This matter is done," and sat down.

Beside me at the counsel table my client shifted her fine dancer's legs restlessly. Sheriff Oldenberg, shrewdly figuring it couldn't hurt him, had let me smuggle her in a mini-skirt and she was fetching in it. She was twenty-six years old. If I remembered rightly I'd once been that age, but the memory was dim—dim. Her name was Mary Ann Moffat and two weeks back the state claimed she'd taken a .38 Smith & Wesson Chief's Special revolver and killed Roger Tuttle with it.

Her hair was long and cornsilk yellow and she wore it down her back like a banner. She was tall and exceedingly well made. She had a sweet voice that could thaw dry ice and blue-green eyes, slightly ex-ophthalmic, luminous and questing. Her father was long dead and her mother was recently dead and she was a little bewildered. She was a handsome child and I knew she was hating her confinement, which seemed about to be ordered by the judge to continue. The numerous times I'd been in to see her in the jail she'd initiated the sessions by holding hands with me, which made visiting her habit-forming. Sheriff "Dutchie" Oldenberg had spied and seen that.

"Son," he said, grinning obscenely, "you'd better watch yourself real close or you're going to get had right out of your lawful fee. Then you'll not only have Boss Watts hot-tracking you, but you'll be working for nothing but a bad case of the early morning back spavins—because that's one healthy filly."

I'd tried to be careful. In a partnership it's difficult to split up that sort of reward successfully. But it was hard to keep things on a purely professional basis. She weakened my knees and she knew it.

Lucas thumped the table, bringing me back to awareness. At his side Joe Watts watched me with eyes that wanted to dissect me, bringing me back to courtroom awareness.

Judge Steinmetz nodded encouragingly. He's the best of judges, impervious to pressure, courteous to all, well schooled in the law, and unflappable. But sometimes at night in these waning days of his life he will call me on some pretext or other and his voice will be faded and lonely and perhaps afraid. There is no longer a Mrs. Steinmetz. Cancer took her years back and late-night television pap cannot subdue his active mind.

He will ask testily: "Are you there, Donald?"

Then he will talk on until the midnight urge dies and the loneliness is quenched for the moment. His voice will become calm and abruptly he will end the conversation.

He is old, but he's very alert and about as senile as a tiger.

There are judges who are judges because of the power or the money. But not Steinmetz.

"Mr. Robak?" he prompted.

I arose. "May it please the court. I think the prosecution has covered most matters. My client, Mary Ann Moffat, is in jail without bond on an indictment charging her with first degree murder. That indictment was returned mostly because of evidence given by Mr. Watts, her once stepfather. He testified here that he believes the defendant to be a dangerously insane person and that therefore she shouldn't be freed because such insanity caused the commission of the act and might be repeated. The matter before the court normally is a simple one in hearings of this type. If the court believes that the presumption is strong or the proof evident that Mary Ann Moffat killed Roger Tuttle then the court may deny bond. If the court feels, on the other hand, that there is doubt or that she perhaps might not be convicted of the crime charged but only of some lesser, included offense then the court may allow bond. So it becomes a case of whether the court believes the testimony of Mr. Watts and his very close companions or does not believe it in full. As to the insanity of Miss Moffat now, we have presented evidence showing her to be sane. We haven't, of course, introduced evidence as to her state at the time of the alleged murder. That we may or may not do at the future trial of Miss Moffat, assuming she is ever tried." I smiled over at Lucas and Watts. They stared back at me stonily. "The only insanity evidence as to that time is the evidence of that expert, Mr. Joseph Watts and the testimony of his associates or hirelings on the fatal day. We presented the testimony of Dr. Hugo Buckner and defend that testimony as to her condition now. He examined her at length recently and testified today that she is not now a dangerously insane person. It isn't my job or Miss Moffat's job to furnish witnesses for the state or allow herself to be examined by the state. I therefore submit that the court has a simple matter before it."

I sat down and looked around the old courtroom where legend has it that the ghosts of long dead members of the bench and bar convened nightly and overruled each other.

Steinmetz nodded thoughtfully. He looked over at Frank Lucas and then at me. "I'm going to deny bond, Mr. Robak. I can't go along with your interpretation of the law. I don't believe that under the law of this state it's up to the court at this time to make a determination that a jury may have to make at some future time. The evidence certainly tends to show that Miss Moffat killed Roger Tuttle in a scuffle for a gun after having opened fire on Mr. Joseph Watts. That's enough to indict her and enough to hold her without bond. The insanity matter is something for the trial, not for me to consider now."

Lucas nodded without triumph. Watts's face lightened a bit, but that was the only sign of emotion from him. At some recess Lucas had probably told him what he'd done in testifying, the doors he'd opened for me, and he was still obviously upset about what he'd heard.

I opened my case folder and got out the motion I'd had Virginia the secretary type. I handed a copy to Lucas and gave the other to the court for filing.

Out in the courtroom the news people and the hangers-on had fled away, but Ted Polly and Alvin Suedell waited, watching me with cold, suspicious eyes.

Judge Steinmetz read the short motion and then nodded. "The motion for a speedy trial appears to be in order," he said. He looked at Lucas. "Do you wish to be heard on it, Mr. Lucas?"

Lucas turned to Watts and they whispered together for a moment.

"Not at this time," he said.

Beside me Mary Ann caught at my hand with anxious fingers. "I don't get my bond?" she asked.

"No," I said. "But they have to start your trial within forty-five days or turn you loose."

I sneaked a look at Lucas. Some of the ramifications of what I was doing were beginning to dawn upon him. He was in the midst of what he knew was going to be a temporary insanity plea, but it hadn't been pled yet. I knew that as time passed other difficulties in his position would become apparent to him.

"When do you want to arraign her?" he asked.

I smiled. "We could do it now and save time if you want. She plans to stand mute."

He clenched his teeth.

I waited for a moment, but he said nothing more and so I turned to the jolly jail matron. She'd accompanied us over each day from the jail and sat patiently with us through the hearing.

"If you'd accompany us back to the jail we'd appreciate it," I said. I turned to Mary Ann. She was watching her one-time stepfather with eyes that brimmed over with malice. I took her arm hurriedly and led her out the side door of the courtroom and down the circular back steps. In that way we escaped the reporters who scurried about the outer hall waiting for any reaction we might express at the decision.

Mary Ann was beginning to recover. We stopped on the last stair landing and the matron smiled at us politely and moved a bit away so we could talk. Mary Ann took my hand again.

She said: "I'd hoped against hope that I'd be in my apartment in a hot soak by now, but not yet I guess." She shook her golden head. "If I shot that poor man I don't remember it, Don, but I've told them that a hundred times. If I shot him I didn't mean to. All I remember is shooting at Joe Watts and then all of them engulfing me." She nodded and fell into thought and finally looked back at me. "At five when you finish in the office I'd really like it if you'd come over to the jail and see me. I feel like I want to go over this mess again and tell you why I believe that monster killed my mother." She waved a slim hand. "I know it's all so foolish and I guess trying to shoot him was dumb, but I was afraid to wait until he got up close on account of the others." She shook her head ruefully. "I messed it up and now that poor man is dead and they say I killed him." She shook her head again. "If that bastard Watts comes around the jail and tries to wheedle me that it wasn't that way I'll make him wish he was wearing cast-iron drawers." She smiled narrowly at me, her eyes a thousand years old. "I don't care what *his* paper reported and I don't care what a coroner's jury decided, where *he* names the coroner. I think he killed my mother. I think he did it because he's got some kind of a sick hang-up on me. And he's almost sixty years old." She looked at me. "Have you noticed how the indignation about this thing is mostly because I tried to shoot him? No one cares about that poor drunk who got killed."

"How old is Watts?" I asked, thinking about the beauty scars.

"He's at least fifty-five," she said, sniffing to show her distaste. She thought about that for a moment and then she noticed me again and her eyes kindled a little. "You come on over at five and talk to me about it some more if you can. I owe you a real, big bunch. The rest of this town's lawyers shied at taking on someone with all the clout he has, but you took him on. I watched him during the hearing, Don. He didn't like what was going on. He's had it his way here in this town. He's going to get even with you for helping me. He has to. I've heard him talk. An eye for an eye. It's his code."

"He got me once already. He helped beat me for office last election."

Her look indicated she doubted that was enough.

In the office Virginia was typing away at flank speed. She nodded at me.

"The Senator would like to see you," she said. "There's no one in with him right now." She gestured me on imperatively.

Virginia is a woman of fifty-odd summers who no longer fights about it. She's a first-rate legal secretary with a better grasp of the law than perhaps half the local bar. We have, as the years have passed, grown able to make allowances for each other. She occasionally complains bitterly about working for both the Senator and me, but she finds fault with every job applicant when we seek assistance for her. And the work gets done. Ably done. Now and then she threatens retirement, but so far the Senator and I have managed to keep her at work. The Senator once told me that I would have to make the supreme sacrifice if she did retire. I must buy her enough drinks to liquefy her mind and then hie her off to a Tennessee marriage parlor. He appeared to be in earnest.

I tapped on the door and then walked on into the Senator's office. He was hot after something legal, taking notes on a dog-eared yellow pad in handwriting no one but he and

Virginia can decipher. He had case books piled in the corners of the room with reckless abandon.

Once he was a state senator for that other party and for a long time before that he was high up in his party's hierarchy. Any man who ever served a day in the state senate is doomed to be "Senator" from that day forward.

His last name is Adams. He's half advocate, half judge, but the whole adds to more than the parts. He has an instinctive ability to delve right to the crux of a murky legal problem and reduce his answer to believability. He's bright and suspicious of easy things and quirky and he's become for me a replacement for the parents I lost early. I believe I've also become the child he and his dead wife never had. Both of us are wary of this relationship, but it's there.

He is, when you get right down to plain facts, one hell of a good lawyer.

He's getting along pretty far in years now. He was never a neat man and his clothes now run from shabby to downright ragged, although the labels are good. I don't think he much notices clothes any more.

When he walks these days it's with a sort of shuffle. He carries pills and I've seen him stick one in under his tongue now and then. There are pain lines in his face that weren't there last year, but he never complains, at least not to me.

He looked up from his book, frowned, and then recognized me. He smiled gently.

"Ah, Donald," he said picking his words carefully, "the repercussions of your hearing are already upon us. Joe Watts called here."

"When was that?"

"This morning before your hearing began again."

"And what did he want?" I asked.

"He was fairly devious for Boss Joe. He said he had some contracts he wanted me to look over." He shook his mane of gray hair. "And here it's been five years since last he called. I'd given up all hope since I'd lost my place in the party." He exposed yellowish teeth in what passed for a smile. "I told him I was too busy these days to take on any new clients. He answered and said that problem might be remedied a bit. Things became chilly between us." His smile became wider. "I therefore came to the assumption that you might have put a crimp in him in court."

"Perhaps," I said. "Our client remains in jail, but thanks to your quarterbacking I have enough evidence in the record to make it about impossible for the three eyewitnesses— Watts, Ted Polly, and Suedell—to change things about her erratic behavior. I'm sure they aren't very happy in the prosecutor's office and I'm also sure they've told Watts why they're unhappy."

He nodded. Heart problems have made all but the most routine of court appearances impossible for him, but they haven't taken the court out of the man. My strategies of the days past had been carefully plotted and looked over by a better lawyer than I'd ever be.

The prosecution was now faced with some bad problems. When we filed our plea of "not guilty by reason of temporary insanity" they could have Mary Ann examined, but if Mary Ann remained mute and refused to answer the court-appointed psychiatrists' questions and we'd already had her examined by our own doctors then there would be only our evidence. At least that was now our theory.

"You understand Watts can be more than a minor problem to you, Donald?"

"I've been up against people with political power before, Senator," I answered, perhaps a little stiffly.

He shook his head and began the lesson. "No one like Joe Watts. He's used to instant obedience around here, to winning, not losing. He might not take any action against you openly, but a mere unfavorable word might starve you down some. His influence is enormous and it extends statewide."

I shrugged, not yet seeing.

His voice was low, but insistent: "You did a term up there in the legislature and so I'm sure you remember that this state keeps a pretty good pad of money here and there, surplus money. Banks hold it for the state and they pay low interest on it. So they make a lot of money by holding it." He looked me over. "And do you do any business with our local bankers?"

"Sure. All lawyers work with and for banks. We check contracts and mortgages for them. We do business with their trust departments. And there are half a dozen other things we do for and with them—probably a lot more than that."

He nodded. "Think about this then. Right now in our three local banks there's slightly in excess of two million dollars in state funds. All those banks probably have some Watts money also. If Joe Watts got real perturbed he might have someone wander into those banks and lay down an edict about you."

"Could he do that?"

He nodded solemnly.

He went on: "Let's imagine he wanted to carry it even further. Pressure might be put on those same banks to put the fear of God in their customers about you, spread the fact that you've contracted a peculiar social disease, and therefore secondarily boycott you."

I swallowed, beginning to see the possibilities.

"The people on the police force and the people who serve as deputy sheriffs might also begin to bad-mouth you."

"If he was the arranger of all that I might just sue him," I said.

He shook his head in negation. "Wrong answer. A judgment, assuming you won one, wouldn't come to a successful flowering for a lot of years. You've seen how those things go—win below, lose on appeal. Besides you probably wouldn't get enough goods on him to even win below. He's a great one for beginning trouble, Watts is. He'd take great glee in the burial of your reputation, but I doubt you'd ever be able to prove he said an actionable word. He'd hold the lantern high and give expert advice about how your interment could be accomplished, but if he heard one little footfall along a side path, he'd blow out the lantern and fade silently away, leaving only judgment proof gentlemen with spades for your recourse." He nodded at me, intent on the matter now. "To go further with your harassment Watts might have arrangements made with his clerk of the court and maybe his recorder . . ."

". . . His?" I interjected.

He nodded. "He elected them. Things might become difficult for you at the courthouse. Records you'd need might become hard to find. The courthouse crew might begin to shake their heads dolefully when your name was mentioned, whisper about your incompetence." He sighed. "Then things might simmer down a little here in the office and Virigina and I could get some welcome rest." He stopped and thought about it, relishing his last idea. "Watts very carefully indicated in our conversation that such plans were in his mind. He's a very tough animal, Donald, and Bington out there is his jungle."

"And what about you, then?" I asked, more worried now. "How bad would it hurt you?"

He rubbed his hands together. "I'm with you, Donald. Most knives are double edged. We'd fight back. Some people would resist his pressure. And I have some friends left in the party. I told him I might discuss such a situation with those friends, perhaps let slip what was happening to the opposition press, dirty him up some. I think that despite all his money he's like most people in his position—he has some interest in a personal political future. At least he probably has the desire to avoid trouble. I doubt we could do him much harm, but he's a cautious man. Something's driving him for him to go this far. And some of the people around him aren't as cautious as he is." He smiled without humor. "I argue better than he does. He got mad finally and hung up on me. But he doesn't like us very well and he'll do *something*."

"As time passes he'll like us even less," I said. "His deceased wife's daughter continues to claim that he killed her mother. That's why she went after him with a gun. She hasn't any concrete evidence and the little I've seen and heard so far seems to show that she's involved in a fantasy and that Watts couldn't possibly have killed her mother."

"What exactly does she have?" he asked.

"Well . . . she says she overheard him talking in his sleep. It convinced her so she got her gun and Roger Tuttle got killed. It's a sort of a mixed-up affair."

He leaned back in his chair. "I used to know Roger Tuttle, maybe as well as anyone ever knew him."

"Oh?" I said. He hadn't mentioned this before.

"He lived out on the lake with his family. There were several kids. One night the house burned. All the others died.

He was maybe eleven or twelve years old then. No one ever got close to him after that. He became a boozer by the time he was maybe eighteen." He shook his head. "Poor bastard. A lonely useless life." He grinned at me. "Kind of like a lawyer."

"True," I said. "I'm going to go to the jail after work and go over it with her again. We'll probably have to defend the criminal charge soon. I filed the speedy trial motion. I've got a feeling that Watts would just as soon drag his feet. I don't think he relishes the idea of her on a witness stand telling *why* she tried to gun him and that she doesn't remember anything plainly after that first shot."

He smiled and I smiled.

"Do you think she might have a convenient memory?" he asked.

"I never examine gift horses," I said. "There's one more curious thing. She told me that Watts, Suedell, and Polly were forcing Tuttle to go somewhere when she took the first shot. At least she thought it was that way."

He picked up his pen. "Interesting if provable." He made a mark on his scratch pad, idly doodling.

"She also says that Watts has shown a more than fatherly interest in her own fair, young body. She makes him sound like a dirty old man. Should make for some interesting days in court."

"I hate to be commercial and crass," he said, "but I assume the young lady can pay us a reasonable fee?"

"Yes," I said happily. "We've already been paid a retainer of one thousand dollars. She can pay for anything we need to do for her. She inherited considerable money from her father's estate plus she now is the sole owner of a multi-unit apartment building which belonged to her and the mother as joint tenants with a right of survivorship. I think it's about twenty units out near the university, plush and unmortgaged."

"Ah hah," he said triumphantly. "There shall be a new bottle of Early Times for the upcoming weekend. And just in time as the cupboard was bare."

"I believe," I said with sorrow, "that Virginia used a bit of the fee to pay the most insistent and distrustful of the book salesmen who feed your habit."

He nodded and went back to his doodling and case reading, dismissing me for the moment.

I slipped out of his office and on into mine and took a seat behind my old desk. I opened Mary Ann's file and poked around until I found what I sought. It was a clipping I'd cut from the local newspaper. It described the death of Mary Ann's mother.

I read it again: "Mrs. Joseph Watts, 43 years old, was pronounced dead on arrival at Mojeff General Hospital of massive head injuries sustained in a one car crash at 4:45 p.m. yesterday near her home on Route Four in the northern part of the county. The accident took place when Joseph Watts, driver of the vehicle, lost control of his late model sports car and it struck a tree near the entrance to the Watts property. Mr. Watts was not seriously injured. The vehicle was damaged extensively.

"Mrs. Watts is the third resident of Mojeff County to die on the highways this year. In addition to her husband, Mrs. Watts is survived by her daughter, Mary Ann Moffat. Funeral arrangements will be announced later."

It was a tasteful little news item. It had been printed on the front page, but hidden a bit in the corner, lower right.

I sighed to myself. What the Bington *Chronicle* did with its news stories wasn't, I supposed, really of any importance to me or to Mary Ann. It was only that I believed that had it been me dead against that tree they'd have given me top left front page with at least a three-column screamer headline. Nothing about Watts's position, only the sketchy accident details, blank as to who'd checked the accident.

Maybe Watts owned stock. The paper leaned his way politically. In fact it almost rolled over his way and played dead politically.

Someone had decided not to make a big story out of the death.

They hadn't let the family anonymity continue. Mary Ann had grown infamous on *Chronicle* news accounts. Reporters and cameramen had plagued us throughout the hearing. In the several news stories I'd seen Mary Ann had usually been referred to as "the baby faced allegedly demented ambush killer." There'd even been an editorial or two. I had a sheaf of clippings from the *Chronicle* and the surrounding big city dailies.

They'd spelled her name right. Mine too.

At five o'clock that night I parked my car outside Bington's old jail. It sat in its half block of space like a Gothic castle.

The jail had been built more than a hundred years back and now the cell doors wouldn't close, the ceilings dripped water in damp weather, and grand juries and jail inspectors blithely condemned it after inspection every year.

Inside a deputy yawned amiably at me and let me into the women's area, where Mary Ann waited for me. Since she'd been in jail, most of the time she'd been the female area's only occupant, although a couple of times one of Bington's female drunks had made it in to keep her weekend company.

She sat awaiting me in the little anteroom that fronted

her cell. A naked light bulb hung down and flooded her dimly with 25 watts. She'd changed clothes. She was wearing some kind of hot pants outfit, ridiculously incongruous in this place, but made for her.

She took my hand as usual and waited until the deputy moved out, closing and locking doors behind him. She drew me on into the inner cell. On dirty gray walls previous occupants had scratched their names plus acid comments about the jail and the world they saw inside it and remembered outside it.

There were three beds, but only one of them was made up. It was covered with flimsy blankets and made up so tightly that a coin might bounce. I threw my coat over the made-up bed to cover it and we took the two hard chairs, both of us embarrassed at being alone and close in these circumstances. I'd talked to her before, but it had been during the day. This time seemed different.

"I hope I'm not keeping you from anything," she said stiffly.

"No. No you're not." I waited.

"I wanted to go over it again."

"It can wait for tomorrow if you'd rather."

"No. I wanted to talk to you tonight." She stopped for a moment. "I know a lot about you, Don."

"What do you know?"

"I know where you go to church, what clubs you belong to, what you like to drink." She smiled and tried hard to forget where we were without really being able to bring it off. "I even know your age."

I smiled back at her in the game we were in. "Then you know I'm quite a bit older than you are."

"Not that much. Within reason I like men who are older."

I remembered Judy St. Avery, my last love at a recent legislative session where I'd served. She'd said she liked men who were a little older, too. She'd said she liked me a lot. She'd given me a gold key chain with a love token dangling from it inscribed: *All my love forever, Judy.* Then, two months after the legislative session was done she'd reconciled with her balding, semipsychotic former husband. She'd called me and confessed tearfully that it was because of her nine-year-old son, but I'd never convinced myself that was her reason. The son had always seemed to be afraid of his father. However there was a lot of inherited money involved and I'd foolishly exposed my own finances.

So these days, just when I'm about to move right up to it and *believe* in something or someone (and particularly around election time when they're promising, promising), I get my key chain out and wave it around in front of my nose and remember that *forever* is only sixty days. And to bolster me I remember my wife who divorced me long ago. I can remember her now with only a nostalgic pang, a bright first date memory of a girl descending sorority house steps into my life. She is not bitch in that memory, but is forever nineteen years old, never to age or change. The wife who left me will grow old, but the memory will always be green and young.

Now, I settled into my hard chair and Mary Ann into hers and we turned toward each other, watching warily. She tucked her splendid legs up under her and I was at a loss for a rejoinder.

"Tell me about Joe Watts," I said, to move it along.

She shrugged and said: "All right. But maybe I should start by telling you something about my mother. She's the important thing." Thinking about her mother made her eyes mist and she visibly fought tears. "She was just a child when

I was born, not even eighteen years old. She married my father before either of them graduated from high school. By all the rules he should have wound up being a check-out boy in a supermarket and they should have grown to despise each other, but it wasn't that way. Pop was energetic, one of those people who generate money. He got into construction. When he made money he kept it. He built our apartment house and he got killed later the same year he finished it. A 'dozer he was running hit some high tension wires and burned him all up." She shuddered visibly, remembering that past bad time, forgetting this bad time in the process. "It took my mother a long time to get over him. She didn't date much. She was selective. Four years ago Joe Watts happened. She wasn't quite forty years old and she looked like she was under thirty. He chased her. He had money and maybe, if he wants, he can be charming."

"Did she ever go with Herman Leaks, the prosecutor?"

"You asked me that before. After things began to break down she did go with him for a time. But it didn't last long. Herman's afraid of Joe Watts."

"Would he have known who she was and who she was married to when he dated her?"

"I don't see how he could have missed it. I suppose it would be possible, but highly improbable."

I nodded.

She looked away from me, remembering. "After I was grown up people used to think we were sisters. We were close. We wore each other's clothes sometimes. The only thing was she wouldn't tell me her troubles. She'd bottle them up inside her and live with them without me ever being able to pry them out of her. Anyway Joe Watts talked her into marriage. She did talk to me about that and I thought it was all right.

They signed a contract so that our apartment building and the money she got from Dad remained hers. If the marriage lasted three years then he had to pay her if there was a divorce. Mother said it was a good business deal. And after they got married it was all okay for a long time." She looked up at me. "I got to know him better and I didn't much like him. Know what I figured when trouble really began?"

"No."

"I don't think he was much man. Big front, plenty of money, flash, but nothing underneath it but meanness. He wanted it all his own way. Mother could get stubborn. I knew when it started going bad. Maybe I knew because they worked so hard at being nice to each other when I was around. Then they even stopped that pretense. She never complained to me, but I saw bruises and twice she had black eyes. I think she still wanted the marriage to work. She must have stayed with him for some reason. I tried to talk to her, but it was like pulling teeth." She looked at me, trying to make me see it the way she remembered it. "Then he got this chance eight or nine months back to take over as state chairman. He was gone a lot after that. I think that's about the time she met Herman Leaks. It seemed to me that things just got progressively worse even with him not being around so much." She looked down at the floor. "A lot of what I'm saying is pure guesswork. She didn't tell me much, like I said. It was like she was maybe afraid to tell me anything." She paused, remembering. "Once when she was very angry at him and uptight I asked her why she just didn't leave. She smiled a little, like I didn't know anything. She said: 'Not yet, not yet.' And then she stopped talking about it."

"Did you live at the house with them?"

"No. About a week before she died Joe called me and asked

me to come out and stay with them for a time. I was worried about her and it seemed like a good way to check up. So I went out. Things were strange. The servants had either quit or he'd fired them. There were just the five of us rattling around in that big house. Joe and mother and me and his two friends, Mr. Polly and Mr. Suedell."

"Was Roger Tuttle around then?"

"No." She stopped to think again, to remember. "Some people would come to see Joe now and then, political people in big cars, some of them with out-of-state plates. Some days he'd be gone. The phone rang a lot when he was around. He spent a lot of time talking to people on the phone, but I wasn't allowed around."

"You never heard anything?"

"No." She rubbed her hands together and looked up at me. "It was easy for me not to see anything. He could hide away from us in his private office. Have you ever seen the house?"

"No, but I think I know where it is."

"It's enormous. It's built back from the road on a lot of land, acres and acres. There's a high fence around it, electrified. The doors are all double lock and bolt things and you can't open the windows from outside the house."

"Did he build the house?"

"I think so. And I think he had the fence built. It must have cost a lot of money." She stopped, trying to recapture her train of thought. "Anyway, things were bad between Mother and Joe Watts. Both of them were drinking too much and they either ignored each other or fought openly. But he was nice to me—nice and attentive. He followed me around. It didn't mean anything to me at first. But he was there all the time. I'd take a swim and bang, he'd be in the pool with me, hairpiece and all. I'd mix a drink and he'd want me to make one for him. He was up when I got up and he went to bed when I went to bed. Mother didn't even seem to notice." She gave me a slanting look, a little embarrassed. "Understand that his attitude didn't mean a thing to me at the time. He never did a thing that was out of line, made no direct passes. He was just *there*. I didn't read anything into it until after my mother was dead."

"It was a car accident according to the papers," I said.

"No. I know what they printed, but she was murdered. Joe Watts killed her or had her killed. He drove his Corvette into a tree near the front gate. He got out of it without getting hurt and she died . . ."

"Where were you?"

"I was in my room. I think it bugged him to have to tell people that I was his wife's daughter. Made him seem too old. There were people coming he said and so I went to my room, but no one came that day except about Mother." She nodded to herself, rationalizing. "I don't know how it was done. Maybe he pointed the car someway and got out and let it hit that tree. Maybe he beat her skull in before the accident. Maybe he was trying to kill himself and my mother. Anyway, he'd have gotten away with it with me, but he talks in his sleep." She realized what she was saying, blushed a little, and hurried on. "Not that I was ever around him in bed, but he drank too much and he got stoned the night she was buried. Sue and Polly had gone on to bed. I don't know what it is, but they're all in something together. Joe went to sleep on the couch in the reception room and I went on to my room. I couldn't sleep and I finally went back downstairs. I heard him then."

Talking about her mother's death was beginning to get to her.

"Easy," I said. "Just tell me about it."

"I remember it all. It was clear. He said: 'I'll get you, Kate. The driver . . . Damn you, Kate. Die!' Then he mumbled some more things that I've thought on and thought on, but never made out. I was frozen there listening. Him moving around half woke him and he sat part way up on the couch. He saw me standing there." She shivered, remembering. "He must have thought I was my mother. He clawed out at me. He said: 'You can't be real, you bitch.'" She lapsed into silence and I waited.

"What happened then?" I prompted.

"I ran to my room. I double-locked the door. He came up and tried to get in, whining around that it was a bad dream, but I wouldn't talk to him or let him in. He gave it up finally. I left in the morning before anyone was up. I only went back the one time. I had a key to the gate I'd kept and I used it to get in. That was after I'd thought about it for a long time. It was when I was going to shoot him and instead maybe killed that poor man, Mr. Tuttle."

"Do you think you might have shot Tuttle?"

She looked away. "I don't know. I don't remember it if I did. They grabbed my hand and someone hit me and I just don't remember."

"All right. Other than for that night when you heard Watts saying what he said, have you talked to him at any other time?"

She nodded. "He called a lot of times."

"For what reason?"

"To tell me it was only a bad dream." She looked around at the jail walls, letting them close in on her, and then back to me. "But he never asked me to move back to the house. Several times he asked me to go to dinner with him, but never to come to the house." She shook her head, considering him. "He's sick."

"Maybe he is," I said. "Is that all the evidence you have?"

"I guess that's it. Not much to have killed a man for, is it?"

"No one's proved you've killed anyone. Maybe he got killed in the fight for the gun and they're covering up for each other."

Her eyes widened a little, taking a bit of hope from what I'd said. I was a little sick. If they stuck to their stories it made no difference.

"It isn't a lot of evidence about your mother," I said. "People have bad dreams all the time and talk in their sleep. What they say doesn't have any connection with the truth or the real world."

"I know about that," she said. She lowered her head a little, not agreeing with me, but trying to be reasonable. "Maybe that's right. But you didn't see him that night. I did. I've thought out all the maybes, added and subtracted, and he still had her killed or killed her. After all that thinking I was sure enough to try to kill him. I realize that trying to shoot him wasn't right or moral, but I wanted something to happen to him. He's got all that money and power. He's arrogant. He thinks there's nothing he can't do." She looked down at the floor. "I have my own nightmares about that other man, Roger Tuttle."

"Just exactly what did you see the night you took the shot at Watts, and Tuttle was shot?"

"I was behind a tree. I was going to sneak in the house, but they came out while I was trying to figure things. I thought

Polly was kind of pushing this other man along, Roger Tuttle, I mean. He seemed like he'd been drinking some."

"Tuttle?"

She nodded. "When I shot the others ducked for cover, but he just stood there. When they saw who it was then Watts stayed back, but the other three came toward me. Tuttle was laughing. I remember he smelled of alcohol when he got up close. They knew I didn't want to shoot anyone else."

"But you don't remember anything about firing the gun again."

"No. I truly don't. When I came back around there were all sorts of police. The three of them said I shot that man." She lowered her head. "I don't know." She got up from her chair and pulled it over closer to mine and took both my hands. "Find out what happened for me, Don. Find out about my mother. I'll pay you. There's money. I can pay for anything you do."

"Maybe I could hire you someone from a private detective agency?" I said.

"No. I trust you. It would be hard for me to trust someone else. I don't think Watts can get to you, but he might someone else." She looked at me and gently massaged my hands with hers. "The sheriff talked to me about you once. He's a sly man and I don't think he likes Joe Watts." She smiled. "He said he'd deny he ever said anything to me, but he said I ought to call you, so I did. He said you'd been involved in some cases that weren't like they seemed on the surface." She nodded encouragingly at me. "He said you were mean and smart."

"That was nice of him," I said.

"Please?"

I thought about it. I was already in partially. It didn't seem wrong to go further. I said: "I'll make you half a deal. I'm going to have to poke around some anyway, check into Watts's background and his friends' background and whatever else I can find. I'll take a look at the accident report on your mother and if anything looks funny then I'll try to go further."

She looked into my eyes for a long moment and then she nodded. It was less than she'd hoped for, but it was enough. She leaned toward me and took her eyes from mine. The bright-penny hair smelled clean and was soft to my touch. She kissed me lightly and then not so lightly so that my vision blurred. I felt like a swimmer caught in the tide, but I'd felt like that before and I had no instant trust in the feeling. I rather figured I was being kissed to seal the bargain, but that was all right.

"One of the deputies might see," she said shyly.

I didn't figure that could be done through the wall, but I stood up and she moved away from me.

"I'd better go now," I said.

She nodded, but her eyes held me there. She said: "Find out for me, Don."

I nodded back. "Remember that you talk to no one about what happened, no one at all. That means not to the sheriff or to one of his deputies. And not to a prisoner. No one but me. Dr. Buckner called a psychiatrist he knows. He'll be down to see you next week. Then you can talk to him." I'd told her before, but telling her again wouldn't hurt.

She lowered her head. "I don't think I killed that man," she said in a low voice.

"That's the spirit."

I went out and got into the Plymouth and drove home.

I live in an old house that's been converted into two apartments. The Coulsons, an older couple, have been in Florida for months.

I have a single door, no other way out.

When I was getting my key from under the mat I saw a strange car parked across the street, a foreign car, long and dark and sleek. Someone sat in the front seat, slouched down, seemingly half asleep.

I went on into my apartment. I didn't leave again that night, although I had one late phone call.

In the morning I walked to the office.

The walk to work was good for the waistline. It sometimes has an additional benefit, unnecessary this morning, but occasionally therapeutic. It removes late night vapors unshaken by tomato juice and coffee black.

I took my usual course through the business district of Bington. That way the frugal downtown merchants could observe me and presume their accounts with me might still be future collectibles.

Bington is now (and will probably always be) "my" town. It's a small and lovely town dropped into the vast puddle of middle America. By sheer luck it's far removed from race riots, cross-country school busing, and the like. At the last election neither political side even bugged the other's headquarters, although both thoughtfully provided a touch of whiskey for thirsty voters who'd "done the right thing."

Bington is distinguishable from a thousand other towns it resembles in size and sleepy character by several things. It is, firstly, a very old town and the ancient brick houses crowd right up to the edges of the streets, like eager watchers at a hoedown. Those houses are sturdy and well maintained and have miles to go before they sleep the ignominious sleep of ghettodom. The early houses are now protected by an array of ordinances and woe betide the citizen who asks for exterior remodeling.

Secondly there is the university. It's a state-supported university. Every year we Bingtonites weather a few protests, streakers, a parade or two, several barefoot, torchlight processions, and perhaps one panty raid. There's also a lackluster football team. But the university, merely by its existence, adds a certain touch of life to the town, so that appears to be a bustling place.

Dr. Hugo Buckner, my physician, whom I much admire, told me once: "Donnie, you've now been here in Bington long enough not to be called a Donnie-Come-Lately, but you have my promise that you'll never qualify as a real residenter on the more cheerful side of your grave."

I remember I nodded in agreement. We were drinking a bit and it was his bourbon.

He continued: "Stay close to your law partner, Senator Adams. He's been around Bington long enough for both of you. Hide behind him should reform come."

I *think* he was joking.

It's a most peculiar town. It feeds upon the university. It stores up further riches from surrounding farm lands, from corn and tobacco. It adds to that from the commerce of the river that lazily borders it to the south.

And to the north of the town the hills hide the rest of the world so that a man is never really positive that the town isn't all there is.

It's an insular area which enjoys its own sins. A certain clique runs the town, and has always run the town, and that's the way it is. Faces change within the clique, but power remains in the clique. Joe Watts runs things now.

I've a good friend who runs a clothing store in Bington: Lou Calberg. Like Dr. Hugo Buckner he's a man I greatly admire. He has value. He's a friend who remains a friend, who doesn't sell you when the market rises or falls.

Once, when we were trying to understand the town after an agonizing time on the golf course, Lou said: "It's not a consciously bad town, Donald. It's not an evil town or a dirty town, but it reacts wrong. It awaits decisions made by whoever has the power and then it abides by them." He smiled. "And it's slow. Even snowstorms get here five years late."

I remember he patted my good, right arm, the one which had helped three-putt four greens, while he checked my appearance. "And get a haircut tomorrow. The barbers need the business now that school's begun again. Try to believe that lawyers should look like lawyers and that they talk a lot in barber shops."

Understand that in my town favors from and for politicians aren't openly for sale. Understand also that we all know there are better ways. There are Christmases, birthdays, almost annual political campaigns, plus secret collections for this and that where debts of honor can be honorably paid. And sometimes, if all else fails, a man can be sold some stock or let in on a real estate deal—cheap!

And so, though things have never been perfect in my town, we all ride along without making waves and hope nothing touches where we touch.

There are and were some good police. George Gentrup, once chief, and good at it, is now retired. He seems a happy man. Coger Rock, the town's best prosecutor in recent times, was succeeded by Herman Leaks last time. Leaks was supported by Joe Watts in the primary. That primary normally settles who'll hold elective office. Coger, always a good trial man, is now coining money as a private practitioner. Herman Leaks drives a Jaguar. The best thing he's done in the office is employ young Frank Lucas.

I don't know Leaks well. Sometimes he seems all right, but there are many whispers. I find it hard to automatically believe in the purity of a prosecuting attorney who drives a Jaguar. It doesn't seem to make much difference to the town about the Jag, but the town has never trusted *any* lawyer and/or politician at rumor hours.

I say nothing about his car. People would look at the Plymouth and say I was jealous. I'm quiet about everything, having been retired to that quiet by public vote last election. It isn't seemly for a defeated candidate to point out interest areas during the off years between elections.

So on this morning I walked to work as I often do, being hailed by friends, acquaintances, and a few enemies.

I thought about Mary Ann as I walked. She was a very lovely girl and I hoped I could help her. Getting her acquitted might or might not be enough. She'd ripped a hole in herself and she didn't even realize the extent of the tear yet. A man had died. Even though she hadn't accepted fully the burden of his death it was working on her. She needed me to prove she hadn't committed that crime or to justify the crime if the former fell through.

It was hard to look at all that lovely girl and say the things that needed saying. But she had enlisted me in her war for a short term, bought whatever weaponry I possessed.

The temporary insanity gambit we were planning was a legally clever move. The Senator had thought of it. But I wondered if it was a real answer? Her conduct might inflame a jury. Such a jury could refuse to believe our proffered testimony, become confused, and convict her. She might be sent to prison. Anything was possible. Maybe we could shake the prosecutor up and deal the matter, plea bargaining for a suspended sentence.

How much pull did Watts really have? A state chairman is an exalted figure. I needed to dig into him *hard*.

Lawyers attack a pending trial situation much like a woodsman axes a tree. Before striking the first blow a spot needs to be picked.

I had a few things going for me. I had the Senator. He wasn't about to be stampeded. I had Doc Buckner. I also had the fact that I'm a despicable bastard, particularly in the courtroom. I've no real desire to hurt, but I rationalize such away with the knowledge that no one should oppose those I represent, who are, after all, fair and right and like that.

Senator Adams has seldom expressed admiration for my abilities to delve into the intricacies of the law, but he has commented several times about my actions in trial situations.

"My," he said, after the first one, "you do come on, Donald," and, after another time: "I believe there's faint hope for you."

This morning I stood out in front of the building which houses our law offices and gazed around me before I went up, admiring my town. Sometimes, as on this morning, I need to pinch myself to believe in the town. It seemed so very clean after the Gary-Chicago that I knew as a child. But then it was early morning and we hadn't had our chance to dirty it up. Yet.

Upstairs, the office door was ajar.

The visitors had done expert work. All our law books had

been ripped from the shelves and lay strewn in torn, tangled piles on the floor. File cabinets had been forced open and the contents of the files scattered. The desks had been ruthlessly swept clean of papers and hardware, the drawers opened and emptied. It was as if mischievous children had declared the office a playground. Even the cords had been torn out of the desk lamps. Over all the room, splashed here, poured there, was black, thick paint.

Virginia arrived while I stood there.

"My Lord," she said. "My Lord!" She took her shabby coat off, but there was no safe place for her to hang it. She clutched the thin fabric tightly in her hands, wrinkling it without knowing what she was doing. She started to cry.

We waited together for a short while, not speaking to each other.

W. Handy Monday, the chief of Bington's police, made the run to the office. He came in and nodded severely at me.

He said: "I've some other business with you, but we'll save it for later, when this is done."

Virginia still cried quietly into her damp, folded handkerchief, but she let it subside and watched Handy with suspicion. She doesn't trust police officers either.

Handy's a new friend. I've known him for a while, but known him well only since George Gentrup retired and took up fishing. Handy's been around Bington seven or eight years and his rise in the Bington Police Department has been meteoric, surprising for a town as political as Bington. There are reasons. Before he moved to Bington he had some years on the Detroit police. He has all the training that a police officer can obtain. He's also very smart. He got to Bington when someone put a bomb in his car in Detroit. He lost his wife and child and it left him a shambles for a time.

We've become friends. There's only so much to do in a small town and only so many people you can do those things with. We've drifted together and occasionally we drink and/or chase girls in tandem.

He's a tall man with a heavy mustache and calm, lake-blue eyes. He must be handsome. He's very popular with the ladies. He's intelligent and once he was a very good semi-pro boxer. He's strong physically. In his office there's a picture I've examined and inquired about. It pictures a younger Handy, *sans* mustache, clad in boxing trunks. The pose is all bravado, straight out of one of the ring magazines, arms at ready, gloved fists up, head erect, shoulders slightly forward. A yellowed newspaper clipping in the corner of the picture proclaims in its headline: HANDY MONDAY NEW PHENOM.

When I visit his office I always look again at the picture. I'm fascinated by the eyes of the man. Then, they were seeking, perhaps vulnerable. Now they are withdrawn and careful, but he wears well. He's become one of the world's great practical jokers, intricate things. Like funny cards that come in the mail from odd places signed in unrecognizable script. Like invitations to parties that never happen. A score of things. Novelty cards, spring snakes made of plastic. He haunts the specialty houses for new ideas.

And yet he does these things anonymously. It's as if he wants the closeness of the joke, but not the closeness of you knowing for certain it was him. No companionship. Distant laughter.

I like him and think he likes me. What I know about Detroit I didn't get from him. He's never said a word to me about his wife and child, about the Detroit years. For all he tells me the world began when he moved to Bington.

He looked around and moved close to me so that Virginia couldn't hear us.

"Could be vandals," he said in a calm, no-nonsense voice. "We had a break in at the high school a few weeks back. Same kind of thing, similar damage." He considered me. "Or perhaps you had a wild party in here late last night?" He noted my sober return glance and said, although we've agreed to laugh at the world: "Sorry. Bad joke."

He walked over to the fire-escape window and I followed him. The window was open. "Probably made entry through the window, then left by the door when they were done." He studied the window sill. There were little dabs of mud on it, red fresh mud. He took an envelope out of his pocket and scraped a sample of the mud into it without making any comment.

"Keep any money around?" he asked, when he was done.

"Ask her," I said. If there was loose money around Virginia wasn't normally going to confide in me about it. She had no trust for anyone on the low side of forty.

She shook her head at his inquiring glance. "Yesterday afternoon I deposited everything. The Senator lets me pay little things out of my own pocket and reimburse myself when it mounts up. Last night there wasn't even any small change in the office."

"Well, it could have been kids," he said again.

"Maybe not," I said.

"Thank you for the expert opinion, Don," he said, not without sarcasm. "Why do you hold it?"

"Where'd kids pick up the red mud you took from the window sill?"

"Where anyone else would pick it up. Maybe one or more of the kids were from a farm or something, maybe one of them walked through a construction area." He shrugged. "I'll want some of my people to come in and look things over and dust for prints." He looked questioningly at Virginia. "Where's Senator Adams this morning?"

"He makes his own hours," Virginia said. "He'll be along." She brought her hand to her mouth, thinking of something. "I wonder if they took anything from *his* office?" She padded quickly into his office. Handy grinned, nodded at me, and we followed.

She sifted carefully through the papers on the floor and looked under the books, taking care not to mess things up even worse in the still sticky paint. Handy and I helped.

If she noticed anything additional missing she said nothing. Handy gave me a nod and a gesture that indicated he wanted private conversation so we left her there and went to my office.

He shut the door and moved close to me.

"I tried to find you early last night," he said. "Where were you?"

"Early? I went past the jail to see Mary Ann Moffat. Not much else."

"What time did you go home?"

I looked him over with more interest. He appeared to really want to know.

"Why are you asking?"

He gave me a steady look. "First thing this morning I received a warrant from upstairs for your arrest. The prosecutor allowed an affidavit to be filed against you for assault and battery upon the person of one Joseph G. Watts." He nodded at me, face serious. "When I got it I went up and told the city judge that if he didn't feel like releasing you on your own recognizance then I'd have to go your bond."

I thought about last night and the man who'd watched from the sleek, foreign automobile.

"And what did the judge say?"

"No bond necessary. At least none yet."

I said carefully: "Thanks for the help, Handy. I appreciate it. Can you tell me when exactly I'm supposed to have committed my crime?"

"I heard eleven o'clock. In addition to Watts there are several other witnesses endorsed on the affidavit." He reached in his pocket and dragged me out a copy. "I had them make this and brought it along to you with the warrant. I thought you'd want it." He handed me both forms. "City judge said to come down tomorrow and talk to him about it."

I nodded. "Okay. I'll come down or call or maybe the Senator will want to do it."

I thought for a fleeting moment about our good city judge. He was a young man who hadn't had an original thought since shortly before he got married some ten years back. He carried out jovially those orders that the prosecutor and the political powers ordered. If one of them informed him that the sun was out on a day it was raining up a storm he'd dutifully have seen the rain from out of his sunglasses. Worse, if he was told that a man was guilty, then that ended the necessity of evidence and the man was guilty, period. He was, however, a nice man of high Christian principles, a member of the Jaycees and drank only the best bourbon. And he was like a pelican in his dealing with Bington's numerous minor criminals, a master fisherman with knowledge of their waters and habits, very good at his job in that way. He was serving his third term.

The accusation of crime was a step up for Watts and friends, a push down toward the gutter for me. I would have to deal with it carefully. It was no time for me to get confidential, even with Handy.

"Thanks for breaking the news to me easy and bringing me copies of the papers," I said.

"No protestations of innocence?" he asked, watching me carefully, smiling a little.

"Not now, Handy."

He shook his head. He wasn't satisfied. He was a very acute person. What sometimes took me a long time was usually immediately apparent to him. So I kept my stare blank. He was a policeman and he worked for *them* and I was a man accused of crime.

"I'll testify as a character witness if you need me," he said simply. "If my word means anything in this town then so does yours. I don't think you did it. I don't know exactly what's going on, but I know you."

"Thanks again, Handy," I said. I felt a touch of shame at keeping my own counsel, but I continued to keep it.

When Handy left it seemed to be a fitting time to go see my friend Lou Calberg so I left the office to Virginia's able stewardship. She'd stopped her tears and gotten mad and efficient. I instructed her to wait for the Senator before allowing her womanly instincts toward order to triumph. The police lab men came up the stairs as I was going down. I imagined they'd heard of my troubles for they eyed me curiously. I figured they might delay Virginia even further, increase her anger, and that she'd be hard to be around for a time. I hurried on.

Lou Calberg runs a clothing store in downtown Bington. He gets stouter, balder, and uglier each year serving Bington's twenty-seven thousand citizens. He wasn't pretty to begin with. He's mid-fiftyish and all of Bington knows, without his publicizing it, that he was a much decorated soldier in one of those wars we used to fight to end wars. Lou has scars and some missing parts to show he was in that war. Once, after a golf game and too much nineteenth hole, we'd showered in the basement of the country club where we fell to comparing scars. His were far more impressive than mine. He's missing half a leg, but he does all right with his fake one. He'd shot a forty-three for nine holes and gleefully taken two dollars of my money that day.

Lou is a man of the Jewish faith. Bington has no synagogue and so he drives to a nearby city for his formal religion. I think that's the only time he leaves Bington.

He's my best friend. I doubt that I'm his best friend, but he's worth sharing and that's all right.

He has many, many friends.

He spends his time in this life running his clothing store, occasionally arguing amiably with his lovely wife, and observing and making mental notes on his environment. He smiles at what surrounds him and has little time for petty things. He's a great listener, a shoulder well known to the town. He is, in my humble opinion, a man who has made peace with the world around him. He's also the town's leading observer.

I thought he might know things about Roger Tuttle and Joe Watts.

I walked down to his store skirting my way from awning to awning to avoid the momentary showers of rain that appeared and vanished as quickly as children playing kick the can in darkness.

His store is very old, one of the oldest on Main Street. He keeps his flawed, old-fashioned windows full of suits and shirts and ties and I looked them over politely before I entered.

He saw me from inside and beckoned urgently and so I went in, smelling the mingled odors of dust, decay, new shoes, and good cloth. It was a pleasant odor. I've accused him of bottling it.

He stumped up to me with his slightly rolling gait. The missing leg makes him walk like a tipsy sailor on shore leave.

"And good morning to you, Donald." He shook his balding head, squinting. I knew he was going over what he'd heard about me recently, deciding what he should say to me.

"I hear you're in trouble with a big man again." He gave my shoulder a pat, trying to be jocular, but concerned a little. He managed to straighten my seam at the same time.

"Who told you that?" I asked curiously.

"I hear it all over," he said evasively. Lou seldom reveals a source.

"Tell me what you know about that particular big man, Lou."

"And maybe Roger Tuttle," he said shrewdly. He thought about it and then shook his head. "You always come around here for your information, but you never come past home these days to see my Rebecca. And you never buy an old friend a drink." He grinned at me and waited.

"So I promise I'll buy you a drink if I can ever catch you sober," I said.

He nodded. "Okay for that, but that don't do it all. You got to come past the house to have the drink. Rebecca asks about you."

"I'll be happy to do that. I wanted to talk to Rebecca anyway about running off with me."

He grinned again.

"Roger Tuttle?" I prompted.

"A dirty man, Donald. A mere touch above the gutter. He'd steal your billfold if you had ten kids. A drunk." His eyes mirrored his distaste.

"He was supposed to have been working for Watts," I said.

"No way. He don't work. He never worked. Maybe you could get him to do some rudimentary things if you fed him enough whiskey. And he'd go out and buy some votes among the other bums on Election Day. Not much else."

"How about Watts?"

He pondered for a moment. "Joe Watts. He's one big man, Donald. People say you shouldn't be trying to get his stepdaughter out of jail after she shot at him. Mr. Watts tells a lot of people what to do. He can hurt you. How are you ever going to wind up rich and with a good practice?" He moved a little closer to me. "But I've seen her. She's a pretty girl." He gave me a sly rib dig. "And she owns property, too. Maybe you can work it out for her and no one will be mad. Then it's time you maybe got married and settled down and had some kids."

He made it sound easy.

"Where'd Joe Watts come from?" I persisted.

"Watts? I've heard he came down from up north. I remember when he came. It was like eight or ten years ago." He snapped his fingers. "It was the year we had the fifteen-inch snow. He was a cheese with one of the auto manufacturers, but something happened. I've heard they forced him out, but he made them pay him a hunk of money. He's worth a lot of millions, Donald." He stopped and thought for a moment. "He dresses cheap, ready made. He buys inferior bourbon, not our good Early Times. He's a poopy golfer without enough friends to form a foursome. No hale and hearty Jug

Hunter. And they say sometimes he don't pay his bills." He pondered it some more. "He does take good care of his cars. Maybe because he was once in the business. He has several cars. The best one's a Rolls you may have seen around town —a yellow one."

I nodded. I'd admired that beauty from afar once or twice. I'd have preferred it in a more sedate color, but a Rolls is a Rolls and Watts might be the type who wanted his car noticed.

"He's also got a new Corvette. They tell me he drives it up and down the back roads at very high rates of speed."

"I thought he wrecked the Corvette?"

"He wrecked one, but he's replaced it. A farmer told me the other day that he saw that car going at about a hundred miles an hour up a narrow, gravel road. He didn't know who was driving." He grimaced. "No wonder he had such a bad accident. I saw the one he wrecked up at Quinn's Body Shop."

"Tell me what else you've heard," I said, seeing I'd warmed him to the subject.

He moved over to a shelf and began to smooth out a stack of shirts with expert hands.

"He's a gross man, Donald. Not in looks, but in the way he does things. Just plain mean."

"What makes you say that?"

"I keep remembering things. He owns a lot of land out north, hundreds of acres. He bought the first big tract maybe a year or so after he got here—belonged to some people down in Lexington who had a tenant farmer on it. Old man named Rossi. Used to come in here and buy his work clothes. Kind of a nice old man without much English. Watts had him served with some kind of legal papers . . ."

". . . A notice to quit?" I asked.

"I guess maybe. Rossi claimed he never was served. Watts hired goons to watch the place and caught Rossi away from it and had his people go in and take over and set the old man out. Wouldn't even let Rossi come back on the place except to get his stuff. Kept guards there all the time. Rossi sued him, but it never came to anything. I think Rossi died before there was a trial. In fact I know he did."

Something ran down my spine. "How did Rossi die?"

He shook his head. "I don't remember for sure. I guess a heart attack. Wait a minute. They found him off the side of a road in his truck. He'd had an attack and wrecked it. A long time ago now. Nothing suspicious about it."

"Except that Mrs. Watts died in a car wreck."

"Lots do." He thought again for a moment. "Watts beat up Sydney Clark one time."

I smiled and he smiled back, thinking similar thoughts.

Sydney Clark's a tiny, little man with a poison tongue. His words are deadly and his mouth wags constantly, industriously. Few Bingtonites have failed to feel Sydney's sting. He's well hated, but most Bingtonites who've made it to adulthood consider it unsporting to do more than try to engage in verbal combat with him. He relishes such encounters, lives for them.

"Smacked him around in the parking lot down at the country club," Lou continued gleefully. "Broke his glasses and loosened up some teeth." He scratched his neck, still smiling. "Way I heard it Watts had played golf with Sydney. Mustn't have known about him. No one plays golf with Sydney except his wife. She's got to be deaf."

"No," I said. "She isn't deaf."

"She should be then. You know and I know that playing golf with Sydney is like toying with a swarm of bees."

"Did Watts do it or did he have one of his friends do it?"

"I understand he did the job personally." He smiled once more and I answered it. Although we observed the unwritten rule about Sydney it was hard to get worked up because someone broke the rule.

"Maybe he can't be all bad," I mused. "You know what Sydney was saying to him that got him so hot?"

"I never heard."

"Speculate for me on why Roger Tuttle would be out at Watts's house?"

"Well, like I said, he was in politics a little. Maybe he was a gopher. A yes man. A fetcher. There ain't any Tuttle kin, Donald. Not even a cousin. Last one in his family and never married. The town might be sorry for him, Donald."

I nodded. It was something to consider.

He waited patiently, knowing I wasn't done.

"Did you ever hear anything about Herman Leaks, the prosecutor, taking out Watts's wife?"

"I've heard it. Everyone's heard it. The whole town. You hear a lot of things about Leaks. I won't repeat them. You've heard them, too. Maybe more than me."

A customer came through the door and he stumped his way toward the counter to wait on him. While he was so engaged I waved to him and went on out.

"Come to the house, and *soon*," he called when I was at the door.

I nodded. Outside I walked on up the damp sidewalk toward the sheriff's office. It was, by now, a typical April day. It had grown warmer and the sun peeked out between clouds. In a few months it would be summer again, the college kids would mostly be gone, and Bington could yawn and relax. Maybe this was the year I'd break eighty and get kicked out of my Jug Hunter foursome for excellence. Then I could give up this legal eagle business and try for my rightful place on the pro tour.

In my next existence I want to be a golf pro on the tour. At first it was a toss up between that and professional football, but I opted finally for the golf. It was a hard choice. Once I believed I wasn't violent enough for pro football, but that was before I experienced politics.

The sheriff of my county is a man named Warren "Dutchie" Oldenberg. He's a nice, jovial fellow of medium size and years. He smiles much of the time, but the smile seldom reaches his eyes. Previously, for many years, he was the operator of a feed mill which did a sketchy business and which he sold gratefully after his election and just prior to his ascension as sheriff.

His early hard times have helped him become the success he is today.

He's now our champion fence-sitter, do-nothinger. He is enchanted with the notion that trouble ignored is trouble that just might vanish. The sheriff's job has become for him a situation of sitting at a big desk in the crumbling sheriff's office and smiling at all comers (but only below the eyes) and ignoring the business at hand. He makes every parade and every funeral. Such conduct has not gone unrewarded. The clean nose resulted in his re-election in the election in which I was defeated. He now looked to me like a man with job security and doing nothing until massive coronary time.

He smiled his meaningless smile at me from his comfortable place behind his littered desk.

"My good friend, Don Robak," he rumbled happily, as if it had been months since he'd seen me. "What service can

I do for you on this fine day? You need to see little Miss Sweetpants again already?"

"Not now," I said. "I would like to get a copy of the accident report where Joe Watts's wife was killed. Can you give me that?"

He wagged his head slowly, signifying nothing, not yet ready to agree or disagree, weighing it all.

"You ain't changed nothing? You're still going to represent our palomino prisoner?" he asked, making sure that he had it all straight.

"Yes sir."

He liked being sirred. He chuckled about it. It was hard not to join with him in shared amusement.

He said: "You still look fit. It must be great to be young and ready. I thought maybe she'd wore you out. My deputy reported you was in with her for a long time last night."

I chuckled with him some more. It was what he wanted and I'm inclined to be a reasonable man. Practicing law can sometimes be a humbling experience.

He hitched his chair toward me, his eyes gone confidential. "Go out and get the desk deputy to make you up a copy. That way I don't know nothin' about it. Old Joe Watts can't get overmad at me. And he do get overmad, Don. He do that." He shook his head mournfully.

"So I should just ask the deputy to make me one?" I asked, wanting to be sure of the procedure.

He nodded, still confidential. "And he'll do that little thing for you unless I specially tell him not to and you'll notice I ain't sayin' nothin'." He stretched and grinned hugely, revealing a mouth full of golden treasure.

"Thanks," I said. I decided to explore him further. I knew he'd never be a real ally, but it seemed worth my efforts to immobilize him as much as I could. "And thanks again for letting me smuggle those clothes in to Mary Ann for the hearing. Some of those reporters like to fractured their eyeballs."

"Good press don't hurt," he said sagely. "But I didn't let you do a thing. Clean clothes ain't against no jail rule I know of—even clean mini-skirts."

"Thanks anyhow," I said. "Mary Ann appreciated it."

He nodded a curt nod.

I moved on with a useful lie: "She said she voted for you last time and would again."

He'd heard the line a thousand times before, but it still pleased him. "I get along with the young ones, Don." He gave me a sly look. "You best talk to the prosecutor about her. I'll bet he'll deal with you, let her off on some lesser charge, maybe manslaughter, two to twenty-one."

"Maybe I'll just do that," I said. "I'm considering trying to work something out." If he was reporting conversations back I didn't want to close the door.

"Talk to him," he urged again.

"Okay. How well did you know Roger Tuttle, Sheriff?"

"Him?" he said disdainfully. "I knew him well enough to have him as a guest here a dozen times. He was a drunk and he was a mean drunk." He looked away from me and his voice became compromising. "Of course that don't give no one the right to shoot him."

"Was he drunk the night he died?"

"Not that I know about. No one said he was."

"Did you ask?"

"He was dead when I made the run out there—by the time I got there, I mean. I smelled booze I thought, but no one said anything. It was open and shut as to what had happened. All three of them guys seen what happened."

"Thanks," I said.

We smiled at each other and I was ready to go on, but I sensed it wasn't time yet.

He looked all around carefully, as if there were a thousand eavesdroppers hanging on each word. He lowered his voice and played one more card from his several decks: "You leave me out of your troubles and your clients' troubles, hear? I don't want to be in no bad crack with Boss Watts. I'll cloud up and rain all over anyone who tries putting me there and I'll do it for a lot of years in a lot of ways."

I nodded. "I guess then you've already heard about my problem. News does move fast in Bington. I won't get you into it, Dutchie. Just tell me one more thing in confidence. I promise it goes no further than me. How close is Watts with Herman Leaks, our prosecutor?"

He shouldn't have answered and he knew it, but he didn't get along with the prosecutor and he'd helped me before in cases where the sheriff's office wasn't involved, given me leads.

He leaned even closer. "They're as close as pancakes and syrup, Don. When Watts wants to hear him a prayer then Leaks is already down on his knees rattlin' beads with folded hands." He thought more about it and gave me a cynical grin. "That's unless he hasn't got his hands up out of Watts's pocket." He nodded, warming to the subject. Then caution decided him against going further. "All this, like we said, is strictly off the record. I never said it. Joe Watts is a very good friend of mine and has been since after the last primary."

I nodded. Dutchie hadn't enjoyed the great one's support in the primary and it still rankled.

A deputy went past the door and looked in curiously.

"Talk to him, Robak," the sheriff ordered, changing his face and hardening his voice like a chameleon moved against a different background. "He takes care of form work. Don't bother me no more about it."

When I had explained and the deputy turned his back to search accident reports Dutchie secretly fed me a wink and gave me one more look at his election-year smile.

The deputy brought me my copy after another moment. I glanced at it hurriedly to make sure it was what I wanted.

The accident had been checked by a number of officers. I spied the name of friend Handy Monday among the names of the investigators. All seemed normal. I folded the report and put it in my coat pocket for closer perusal at a later time. I also decided to discuss the accident with Handy.

Around the courthouse, in neat, geometrical beds, a few flowers were beginning to poke frost-suspicious blooms out. A jail prisoner-trustee hoed unenthusiastically at the flower bed borders and stopped to watch me with eyes that were dying as I went by.

At the office the Senator had arrived. He sat in his room and surveyed the wreckage.

"Someone had this purposely done," he said to me darkly.

"Yes."

"The timing makes one man very suspect."

"Yes," I said again.

He shook his head. "Sometimes I wonder about people. So damned many of them are flawed and useless. Now I'm going to have to get in the act and cause some problems." He looked down at the floor.

"How do you mean to get in the act?"

"I'm just going to make a few calls. Maybe the governor. Build a fire or two." He looked around again. "This can't really hurt us and I think he's smart enough to know it. There's insurance. I already spoke with the insurance people and they told me to go ahead and do what had to be done and send them the bills. So all that happens is we're inconvenienced." He looked up at me, his eyes bright and hot. "Theorize for me why the simple bastard had this job done?"

"He's showing us his power," I said. "I pulled his tail a little in court and maybe it made him angry. No one's supposed to represent those people he wants to get. He's a direct man. It's a fault at times. He took action in maybe several ways and this was just one of them. He also signed and caused to have filed against me a charge that I assaulted and battered him, in case you hadn't heard yet."

He raised his eyebrows. "And did you assault and batter him?"

"Nope. Not unless I drank too much at home and drew a late blank and I didn't. But he believes he has me. He had someone watching my place last night and he knows I didn't go out. I have no alibi. The neighbors in the other apartment are still in Florida so it will be my word against the collective word of Watts and friends."

"I assume you've been arrested?"

"After a fashion." I waved my hand. "There are reasons why I don't want to raise any issues about the form of arrest."

He gave me a quizzical look, but nodded when I said no more.

"Is a hearing date set?"

"I promised to contact city court tomorrow. I'd like for you to enter an appearance for me and file a motion for a change of venue from the judge and a trial by jury. That should slow things down a bit."

"All right." He pondered it some more. "If I know Watts he'll continue to push Herman Leaks to set it for trial."

"That's to be expected," I said. "I want to appear to be reluctant to have it set, but I want it tried."

"Okay," he said. He examined me carefully, knowing there was something I wasn't telling him, but willing to wait for it.

"Do I get to try it?"

I shook my head. "No, but I'll appreciate you doing the preliminary work."

"Yes," he said. He moved a little toward me. "Watch yourself, Donald. I smell a mess boiling in the Bington political kitchens. I don't know what's in the pot, but maybe I can find out. But you watch it. A turn of the wheel and your health is gone, a few days pass and you're old. I intend to help. I'll be there at the trial."

I shook my head, but he only smiled and turned away.

I went on into my own office, moved my chair where I wanted it, and sat down, feeling the good warmth within me that had come from our shared conversation.

Yesterday I'd finally gotten to question Joseph G. "Boss" Watts after a long direct examination. In that direct examination Watts had stated that his former stepdaughter, Mary Ann Moffat, had delusions and suffered from bad dreams, exhibited an insane look in her eyes and upon her features the night she'd tried to kill him and killed Roger Tuttle, was unstable, withdrawn, and sullen for weeks before the attack, had attacked her mother on several occasions before that "dear lady" had been accidentally taken, and had fought like a deranged person when she was disarmed after killing "poor Roger."

It seemed to me that he was trying to hand me my defense.

Deputy Prosecutor Lucas had turned him over to me with badly concealed reluctance. There's a term for witnesses like Watts in the legal trade. They're referred to as "blabbers."

I would have bet a bunch of money that Lucas had warned Watts about going too far, about overstating facts, about overkilling the situation. But some people, including some bright ones, once they mount the witness stand, lose control. Watts had visibly been one of those. He'd been well rehearsed, almost unctuous. He'd had dignity, aplomb, and plausibility when he began. And he'd gone on and on and on until it was gone.

What he didn't know was I had Dr. Buckner still to testify. Buckner was, among other things, Mojeff County Coroner and County health officer. I'd seen him when I first began visiting Mary Ann in jail. I'd covertly asked him to examine Mary Ann and had her fake headaches for a reason. The Senator had suggested doing it that way, knowing Bington better than I'd ever know it. And somehow, perhaps because the jail was run apathetically and the sheriff and prosecutor didn't get along, the word miraculously hadn't leaked. Buckner had stated to me on the phone twenty-four hours before that no one from the prosecutor's office or from anywhere else had contacted him.

I'd not had him dig at her about the death of Roger Tuttle or what had happened around that time. I'd had her state to him only that she hadn't, to the best of her knowledge, killed anyone.

But I had gotten him to examine her so that he would be prepared to state her mental condition *now*.

Having that waiting I went to work on Watts.

I stand away from a hostile witness so that in looking at me his face is visible to a jury. If there is no jury then I stand so that the judge can see the face of the witness.

The judge knew what I was doing, but I didn't think that negated the value.

"Was Mary Ann Moffat staying with you at the time you say she shot at you and Mr. Tuttle was killed?"

"No, sir," he said. He eyed me confidently. He had no fear of me. He'd spanked me good in the last election and that victory had decided him as to my worth as an opponent. He smiled and waited. I thought he was a vain man who really only heard well the sounds he himself created. I moved closer to him and noticed the scars at his ears again. He'd had a face lift so he could remain pretty.

"But she did stay with you and her mother at your home for a time before Mr. Tuttle was killed?"

"Yes. She left my home after her mother was tragically killed in the auto accident."

"She moved right after the death of her mother?"

He nodded. "Yes. She acted strangely. She could have stayed at my house. I wanted her to stay. She accused me of having something to do with her mother's death. It became apparent she needed help, even back then. She wouldn't allow anyone to help her, though." He turned to the judge. "I was already asked about this before."

Steinmetz smiled amiably. "Within reasonable limits, Mr. Watts, it's Mr. Robak's privilege to ask again."

Watts shook his head at such legal foolishness and waited for me to continue with ill-concealed dislike.

"Was she having those delusions you testified about while she was living in your home, Mr. Watts?"

"Of course."

"Please describe them for the court?"

He concentrated on that for a moment and then said: "She acted quiet and dreamy around the house most of the time. When she was in that sort of mood she sometimes thought things were different than they actually were. She thought my swimming pool, for example, was a lake she'd lived near when she was a child. Sometimes, in that mood, she'd stay almost all of her time in bed, just lay there. We'd have a hard time getting a word out of her. Her mother said a lot of times that she needed treatment."

Mary Ann gave me an urgent sign.

"One moment," I apologized.

She whispered: "Mother used to call the pool 'Lake Pleasant.' It was a gag thing between us. We laughed about it. He knows that. He knows it didn't mean anything."

"All right," I said. "Let him go on. I'm almost sure they know nothing about Dr. Buckner. They don't believe we have any testimony. Normally there isn't any."

"How do you mean?" she asked dubiously.

"I mean that normally the defense doesn't present any evidence and that hearings like this are held so that the defense can hear the state's evidence."

"Oh," she said.

"No more interruptions," I said. "Let him have his moments now. I want to get him on the record with all the pseudo-psychology I can get."

She nodded, hating Watts with her eyes. I squeezed her hand and went back to my station.

"I believe you also stated that Mary Ann suffered from bad dreams, Mr. Watts?"

"Yes," he said. "She'd toss and turn at night. We could

hear her. A few times she fell out of bed. And she talked in her sleep, gibberish mostly. Then once she went to sleep out by the pool and fell off the chaise longue. She was screaming something that I never could make out. She was badly frightened when she woke up on the concrete. She didn't know where she was."

"And these things just got worse and worse, got more frequent?"

He was reluctant not to supply an answer. "I suppose."

"I remember you also stated she had dark moods and at times like that she was dangerous to those around her—particularly her mother?"

"Yes. That's the way it was. Those times were impossible to predict." He shook his head, the picture of puzzlement. "Even her mother couldn't tell when one would strike. Yet sometimes Mary Ann could be very sunny and winning. Then, like quicksilver, she'd change and do some cruel thing, usually to her mother, strike her, pinch her." He looked down at the courtroom floor and lowered his voice. "Of course it was absolute hell for me."

I stopped and his eyes came up, waiting and watching, contemptuous of me, but hiding it. Assuming that some of what my client had told me was close to the truth then his testimony was quite clever. He was blaming Mary Ann for the many things Mary Ann claimed he'd done. And he was the one with ownership of the eyewitnesses. Pretty good.

"Describe for the court her actions again when she tried to shoot you and killed Mr. Tuttle, Mr. Watts?"

"I retreated—ran if you want to put it that way," he said, smiling. "I'm not ashamed. It was obvious that I was her quarry. She missed me with her first shot and I saw no future in giving her a better opportunity. So I ran. I had Mr. Tuttle and two other associates with me. I wanted them to run also, but they didn't run."

"Did you order them to run?" I asked.

He shook his head. "No. They thought they could talk her out of the gun. She made them fight her for it."

"Did you see her shoot the gun at Mr. Tuttle?"

"Yes. I wasn't that far away. There was a struggle for the gun and then I heard the shot. Mary Ann and Roger both fell."

"Who had possession of the gun?"

"She had it." He looked away from me. "I guess she fainted after she shot Roger. I've heard she says she doesn't remember what happened." He gave me a narrow look. "There's something wrong with her head."

"Were you and your other friends forcing Mr. Tuttle to go someplace when she started shooting?"

For just a tiny instant his eyes widened. "Certainly not."

"What was he doing at your property?"

"I'd hired him to work for me—just general work—housecleaning, handy man. Poor devil needed a job." He shook his head. "I'm sure you know he had a drinking problem."

"Had Mr. Tuttle been drinking that night?"

"I'd imagine he had. I didn't see him drink anything, but he almost always was into it."

"What did you do after the shooting?"

"Called the police. She was arrested. She was either still passed out or feigning it when they came."

"I see," I said, trying to make him think I believed it, trying to be shocked about the whole thing. Sometimes you can build a temporary rapport with a hostile witness that's valuable, but he watched me from a far spot, not falling for it a bit.

"About how far was she from you when she first fired?"
"Quite a ways. I'd say fifty or sixty yards," he said.
"When she shot at you then you immediately believed she was having one of her periodic irrational spells?"
"Yes. She acted crazy."
"You could see a wild look in her eyes?"
He solved that one. "On her face," he corrected.
"And you thought she was shooting at you and your associates because she was an insane person?"
"Yes," he said. "All she needs is a good doctor to examine her and treat her. I talked to a good doctor about her and he'd have examined her and treated her if you'd have let him."
"Yes," I said.
Watts waited triumphantly, having made his point.
"You're very sure then that any doctor would discover she hasn't been sane for a long time and isn't sane now?"
"Of course."
"And everything you've stated here about her is the complete and absolute truth?"
He gave me his best, shocked look. "Yes, sir," he answered stoutly.
I let him go and called Dr. Hugo Buckner.
Joe Watts listened and grew red and angry. Buckner categorically testified that Mary Ann was now sane and no risk to be placed on bond.
But there'd been no bond. I really hadn't thought there would be bond set.
All I'd really shown was that Watts was a poor psychiatrist.

Around noon I left the office for lunch. I decided to eat at the Oasis. Sydney Clark often ate there.
The office smelled of paint. Two boys that Virginia had

managed to hire worked diligently at cleaning and reshelving under her imperative eyes. The police had vanished.

"When may I expect your return?" she asked.

"Probably around two o'clock," I said.

We nodded briskly at each other, two soldiers who'd managed another morning's battle. We'd never be friends, but this day we were at least comrades in arms.

I walked out into a pretty good day. The rain had vanished and the sun was full out. The air smelled of growing things. I decided to walk all the way out to the Oasis rather than take a bus. It was a ways, near the university, but there was time. There usually is time in a small town.

I walked. It was eight blocks, a pleasant journey. Coeds crowded the sidewalks and I looked them over with practiced eyes. The crop was quite fine this year. Somehow it seems that as world problems worsen the women grow more beautiful, so that there are other things to think on, night and morning, than news headlines.

For the thousandth time I debated vaguely within myself about taking off my suit, putting on jeans, and growing a beard. I could then dive back into the life of the university and fall away from the rest of it. A *guru*. The easy life.

Instead, I girl-watched.

And, on the far side of the street, trying to be inconspicuous, I saw someone familiar. He was either just going my way or I was still being watched. Polly. Ted Polly, friend of Joe Watts, witness to assaults and murder. I hesitated and looked pointedly at him and he stopped to check out the merchandise in a store window. The window was full of female apparel.

I smiled and moved on. For some reason they were still interested in what I did and who I saw.

The Oasis has been, for many years, my nominee as the best bar in Bington. They keep it dark and quiet inside. The prices are high enough to discourage bargain hunters and most problem drinkers.

I went in and looked around.

He was there. At a table, all by himself, with empty tables surrounding him, sat little Sydney Clark. He was hunched industriously over a bowl of chili. A huge cheeseburger awaited. Sydney was talking to himself between bites. He does that when there's no one else to talk to. Someone who once overheard said he raises hell.

I sighed without pleasure and walked on back.

"Can I sit with you, Sydney?"

His eyes flickered to empty booths and tables and he was surprised. He grinned knowingly, figuring I wanted something from him. He mentally sharpened his fangs. He hated all the rest of us, but he had a special place inside the Bunsen burner of his heart for doctors and lawyers. I knew I was meat on the table.

"You want my billfold now or when we finish?" he began, mildly enough.

"I wanted to talk to you about Joe Watts," I said.

He nodded and added and subtracted. "I heard you were up against him. It's all over town. I'll even talk to a bastard like you about a bastard like him. He needs to have it happen to him." He smiled cherubically. "Maybe cancer of the brain or a bad stroke. I'd sue him, but it's public knowledge that any lawyer around this town would sell me out for a half dollar." The smile widened. "You'd do better. Your going price is a quarter."

"Why'd he hit you, Sydney?" I got in.

He shrugged. "I'm not for sure. I wasn't doing anything.

I asked about his wife and her daughter. I was working at being nice. I said something about them being attractive and that they looked like sisters. Just remarks passed on the golf course. I tried to help him with his game. He's bad, Robak. Worse than you. He never said anything, never acted angry. But when we were done he waited until we were close up to his two friends and then he smacked me." He nodded. "Did it like you'd do it, Robak. Without warning. Legal ambush. Can't take a little conversation." He nodded again, this time morosely, not really understanding the world around him, but wanting to understand it.

While he pondered I took a quick look around the bar. At the bar on a stool and with his broad back to me was my follower, Ted Polly. He was seated so he could check us out with a turn of his head.

I turned back to Sydney. "Do you remember the last thing you said to him? The thing that set him off?"

He shook his head. "I thought about it after. Last thing I remember was kidding him about that Corvette. I saw one once that had been in a minor accident. The Fibreglas body looked like someone had taken a lawnmower to it. I think I said it was something like driving a hearse. I was just kidding. And he slugged me. The bastard."

"Was that before his wife was killed?"

"Of course. You think I'm insensitive or something?"

I shook my head and he waited. The information was interesting, but knowing Sydney, it was possible that something he'd said before on the golf course might have been what set Watts off.

"Your main problem is that you're basically a very offensive person," I said to Sydney, rewarding him with the insult he wanted.

His eyes narrowed and brightened. It was opening enough. He said: "The world of man first learned about you lawyers from your patron saint, Cain. He dismissed his brother's case. Down the path we also find Julius Caesar. He was, of course, a lawyer. Those weren't fits he had, but mere practicings for arguments in front of some bought Roman jury." He began warming to it, getting up a head of steam. "Brutus probably put the knife to him for failure to split a fee. And so it's continued. Now, before anything good ever happens again, all you lawyers will have to be executed. My method would be to put you all in one huge, foodless arena and let you take a vote on who is to die first. I'm sure you chunks of manure would make it an honor of some kind, *going first*, set up committees to research candidates, appeal decisions, file motions to set aside, demur, and all die of hunger before any person is named first for execution. But, if it would work out someone would be named first, Robak, I'd hope it was you. You were my own favored candidate last year when the Skunk Hollow Yacht Club was trying to decide on a victim for their annual benefit drowning."

Sometimes, when he gets going well, we who know him have observed little white specks of froth come at the edges of his mouth and seen his eyes bulge slightly from his head. He doesn't hear other voices when he's rolling good, just drowns them away by raising his own voice and by increasing the speed at which he shouts. Nothing registers at all.

Today was only practice. He even stopped for a long breath and a cheeseburger bite.

"We lawyers are all nice fellows, Sydney," I said in the unexpected silence. "We're merely misunderstood by a general public made up mostly of clowns like you."

It triggered him further up the line. He got into my ancestry, all the way back to Judas, then traced me forward through a line of progenitors whose least crime was horse thievery. His language grew more pungent.

A sweet young waitress took my order. I smiled at her, but Sydney continued straight on through our conversation, with the waitress blushing now and then at his smokier statements. She scurried away and brought my order on the run, dropping a bowl of soup and a cheeseburger as she went by at high speed.

At quarter to one Sydney checked himself, looked regretfully at his watch, allowed me one more blast, and got up.

"Got to move now, Robak," he said affably. "Nice to eat lunch with you."

I nodded dazedly and he left. I thought on an additional danger from lunching with him. He has a tendency at times to say something nice about someone who's been on the receiving end, as I'd been this noon. Having Sydney say something nice about you made you open to immediate suspicion from all who heard it.

I shook my head and finished my cheeseburger, my ears still ringing a bit. Sydney had a nice little wife who'd tuned him out years ago. There weren't any young Sydney Clarks, there's a pity.

There was still Ted Polly to deal with. It was a point of interest to me that I was still being followed and/or watched. I supposed I could ignore it, but I decided not to do so.

Besides I knew Polly. I'd known him first when we were small boys. *Then*, he'd been a little dough lump, always ready to run, a constant joke in the tough section of Gary I'd lived in. *Then*, he'd been incapable of friendship, of giving or receiving anything of people value. There was too much fear in him. He'd been a fat animal caught in the trap of school, not swift enough in the head or heart to find his place.

We'd moved away and I hadn't seen him for a long time.

When I saw him again we were grown men. He'd changed, at least outwardly. Something, or perhaps someone, had put him on the body-building, muscle-man kick and he'd found refuge there. He'd built biceps and triceps into impressive masses, but his eyes looked out warily at the world, still bewildered.

I took the seat next to him at the bar. When he ignored me by looking the other way, I tapped his shoulder.

"Hi, Polly," I said cheerfully.

He turned to me trying to keep his face innocent. He was a poor actor.

"Hi, Don," he said, shaking his head as if to clear it and clutching at the edge of the bar with massive fingers. "When'd you come in?"

"A while back," I said and waited.

"I just come in to grab a quick beer," he said. He patted his abdomen. "Can't drink much without this all going." He tapped it again, narcissistically liking the feel.

"Didn't I see you last night?" I asked.

"Oh sure. At Mr. Watts's. Too bad about that, Don, but maybe you and him can get together and straighten things out."

"Maybe we can at that," I said. "But I thought I saw you near my apartment last night. Just when I went in." I gave him my best innocent look. "Did you see the girl I had waiting for me there?"

He grinned, solving me. "You didn't see me, Don. Not me. And you didn't have no girl I'll bet. Not last night."

I decided to give that gambit up for the moment.

He smiled and said: "I still remember you from grade school, Don. You were a good guy. I remember once when them black guys ganged me and you got into it and made them leave me alone." He nodded. "Maybe you forgot, but I remember. You were a good guy."

I didn't remember, but I nodded.

He got up from his stool and laid a heavy hand on my shoulder. "You talk to Mr. Watts, Don. I'll bet you and him can get things all straightened out. He can help that Mary Ann. I know he don't want her hurt."

"Tell him to quit having me watched," I said. "Tell him that I've got some witnesses to the fact that he has been watching me."

"Sure," he said, maybe knowing I didn't have any witnesses. He patted me heavily on the shoulder, still not angry, and turned away, walking with the curious grace of the heavily muscled.

I paid and walked back to my apartment. If Polly was still following me I saw nothing of him.

At the apartment I got into my Plymouth, crossed my fingers, and pushed the starter button. The warm weather had improved its health. It started.

I need a new car and know it, but the last time I tried for a trade and had asked what I'd be allowed the salesman-comedian told me to take the Plymouth down a dark street, cover its headlights, and shoot it in the motor. When I'd persisted in my madness he'd politely asked me what it weighed.

The Plymouth has a number of problems. The brakes need relining, the motor is shot, and it uses a lot of oil. The driver's seat belt is screwy. If you touch it anyplace to the right of the buckle the buckle drops off.

It has one virtue. It's paid for.

I drove to the office and parked there. Inside all was quiet. Virginia was out to lunch and the Senator wasn't around. I made a few phone calls in answer to messages Virginia had placed on my desk and then decided to go past and see my friend Dr. Hugo Buckner.

His office is a short block from mine and is hard to believe. There are five treatment rooms and he's staffed with a covey of nurses, a receptionist, and a full-time bookkeeper. Inside his office Doc runs from treatment room to treatment room handing out mostly words and aspirin. His patients seem to thrive on such treatment. He looks like a doctor and maybe that starts him ahead. He's thin, a little older than I, has a wife and several children. The best thing about him is that he has an offbeat sense of humor.

I gave my name to his haughty receptionist, sat among the sufferers, and waited until I was called to one of the treatment rooms. After a while he came speeding into my room, saw me, and slowed a little.

"Drop your pants," he ordered. "A series of penicillin shots will fix you up as good as new. No worse than a cold you know. Of course I'll have to know the names of your contacts for the public health people. Write them in this little black book."

"I'm not dropping my pants," I said with feigned belligerence. "I've told you before that I'll take a drink, but I don't go for any of that upstairs funny stuff. Go chase a nurse and try to act normal."

"I'm trying to quit," he said, grinning. "I heard your hearing didn't come out so well."

"She's still in jail, but the outlook's improved. I'm supposed to thank you for testifying for her."

"She seems like a nice kid." He thought for a moment. "I heard about testifying against my esteemed party leader after the hearing."

"Oh?"

He nodded solemnly. "I got a call and was informed I'd committed a naughty-naughty."

"And what did you say to that?"

"I told my caller I was sure gee-whiz, gosh-awful sorry about doing something that wrong."

"Who called you?"

"A male voice. Mr. Anonymous. He wanted to know if I hadn't made some kind of a bad mistake under the circumstances. Kept returning to that. Was miffed when I kept answering in the negative."

"You being the coroner and all how well do you know Joe Watts, Doc?"

"Not very well. I was out at that big fortress he calls home once for a reception for some congressman. I only just got there and was trying to figure out where they hid the silver when someone came down with an emergency cold and I had to leave." He nodded his head in admiration. "He's got quite a place out there. A lot of land. Been putting it together for a long time, I guess. Couple of thousand acres and wants more."

I hadn't realized there was that much land and I wondered why there was so much.

"What's he raise?"

"I don't know. Crops, I guess."

I switched subjects. "Did you examine his wife Alma after she was killed in the auto wreck?"

"Yup. She was dead when I arrived at the scene. Massive head injuries. When the car clipped the tree stump she obviously wasn't belted in. Her head hit the window and the front-door post."

"How do you know that?"

"I don't for sure. I theorize. There was blood on the door post. I guess Watts had on his belt and harness, but she hadn't put hers on. The force of the crash must have lifted her up into the front glass and that right-door post and smashed her head apart the way a kid would break a melon throwing it against a wall. No other injuries except a dislocated right shoulder and a fractured arm. Lord knows how those came about." He grimaced. "You take a car at high speed and a lot of peculiar things can happen in a crash." He looked up at me. "You read in the papers last week about the one where those three folks from over in Illinois got killed?"

I nodded, remembering. "The one on the interstate?"

"Yeah. That one. There was a two-year-old in the car who got away without a scratch. When the truck came across the median and hit them head on I think the child got thrown clear out an open window and onto the grass. It was cold and a little slick that night and he had on rompers and a coat and he just hit right and slid right." He gave me a somber look. "Cute little kid. I saw him at the hospital. Very bright and talkative, but every time his door opened he looked up sure it was his folks or his sister come to get them. Grandparents finally came for him."

I nodded and we were quiet for a moment. There's an army of kids in like circumstances out there living on social security and insurance settlements. The army grows and grows. To get too deeply involved in the special problems of the survivors is to open yourself to hurts that can't be remedied.

To end the silence I said: "Can I have a copy of your autopsy report on Mrs. Watts? And I'd also like to have one of the late deceased Roger Tuttle."

"All right," he said. "I've got a special girl here in the office just for things like that. All she does is make copies and keep files for my good old Uncle Samuel. She's also a competent belly dancer, but I only let her do that in the dark of the night." He nodded, smiling to himself, his agile mind moving on, losing the need for me as an audience. "You stay here. She'll bring your copies." He slapped himself smartly on the haunch. "Giddeeup, Horsie." And he whirled away.

I waited. In a while a harried girl brought a copy of the autopsy reports on Alma Watts and Roger Tuttle. I stuck the copies in my inside coat pocket along with the accident report.

I figured by now that Joseph G. "Boss" Watts, what with his watchers and all, would know I was still digging at him, trying to find niches in the armor. Ted Polly would have reported in, someone in the sheriff's office would have called.

I went back outside and walked to the Plymouth and recovered the seat with an old blanket I use to keep the seat stuffing from sifting through the worn lining and onto my clothes.

It was getting late in the afternoon so I decided not to climb the steps again. I drove down by the river and sat there, watching the broad, muddy waters. It was in flood now and the water was dark brown and full of drift.

I took the various reports from my pocket and looked them over, first things first.

The coroner's report on Roger Tuttle wasn't of much value. He was forty-six years old and had no permanent address. He'd died of a contact gunshot wound—the bullet having pierced his heart. According to Buckner death had been instantaneous. An autopsy had been performed. Prior to his death he'd suffered from a slightly enlarged heart and from what I translated to mean cirrhosis of the liver. His blood had tested .24 alcohol, well over the presumptive intoxication line.

So he had been drunk . . .

I put it back in my pocket thoughtfully and spread open the reports on Alma Watts.

Translated, Doc Buckner's coroner's report stated that Mary Ann's mother had died of massive head injuries. She'd also, as Doc had said, suffered a dislocated right shoulder and a compound fracture of the two bones in her right forearm, the radius and the ulna. Buckner also listed probable internal injuries.

The accident report I'd secured from the sheriff's office was more complex. It had been prepared by my friend, W. Handy Monday, which seemed unusual until I thought about it for a moment for the accident had happened in county territory, not city. But I remembered that the good sheriff had deputized all of the city policemen and often used them for accident runs, especially those where he believed votes couldn't be easily attracted.

The report was on a standard form drawn up by the state police. It gave the date and time of the accident, make of vehicle or vehicles involved, names, amount of damage as estimated, injuries, etc.

The day had been sunny, the road dry. The time had been 11:30 A.M. and no witnesses to the actual accident were listed.

Under disposition of vehicle the report indicated the damaged Corvette had been removed by a wrecker to Quinn's Body Shop. I wondered if it still was there.

On the back of the form there was a printed map upon

which the investigator could pen in, upon an imaginary road, his decision as to what had happened. The drawing showed a tree on the side of the road, a car against it, skid marks indicated behind the car for 130 feet, and arrows showing the direction the car was traveling before impact. All of this was in Handy's careful hand.

I looked it over several times, but nothing inspirational came.

I sat there for a time looking at the river. I knew my problem. Watts had the Indian sign on the town, maybe on the state. I might make him uncomfortable looking into him, but he knew there wasn't much I could do.

When I next looked at my watch it was after five o'clock, the witching hour for poor, tired lawyers. I'd piddled away another day without notable success.

The weather continued warm when I went to the sheriff's office after a solitary supper consisting of a double hamburger and black coffee at the Elks. While I ate, the early drinkers eyed me from the bar and reminded each other of the squib the local paper had run about my arrest for crime. No one came over to talk to me.

Outside the sheriff's office the hangers-on were only slightly more friendly. They sat on benches and watched the street, discussing the town. I nodded and things cooled down a little, grew more quiet, maybe careful.

I wasn't offended and visited with a man who was willing to talk.

A young girl in a micro-mini strode by. She seemed also to be without brassiere. She smiled at all of us as she went by.

My acquaintance said, leaning on his three-pronged cane: "Soon they'll wind up completely naked."

We smiled at each other, but some one of the other loungers shushed him before harm could be done.

The girl quickstepped on.

I went on inside, hearing the conversation behind me intensify, hearing my name once or twice, as I moved away and to the door of the jail.

A different deputy escorted me back to her cell, tapped on her door, and waited with me, smiling knowingly.

She was wearing a blue dress with just enough green in it to blend with her eyes. I knew she'd dressed for me and I had a little pang of sadness that she'd done that, for it seemed to me false that she should do it.

The deputy lost his smile and looked her over, slightly bug eyed. He nodded appreciatively at me and reluctantly retreated.

"Do you need anything?" I asked.

She shook her head. "I'm having my meals brought in. They do that for you if you can pay."

She led me into the inner cell and once again, warily, we took our accustomed seats. This night I'd worn no coat and the bed got no additional cover.

"I thought of some things I wanted to ask you," I said.

She waited, watching me, smiling a little, so that it was hard for me to think.

"Where did the gun come from?"

"It was my mother's. She kept it in a drawer in the apartment. I guess it was Dad's before it was hers."

"Did anyone ever teach you anything about shooting?"

"No. You see things on television."

"All right." I didn't want to get into trial and have the state start proving she was some kind of expert marksman and me not know anything about it.

"You ever shoot the gun before that night?"

She shook her head.

"How would I go about getting a copy of the agreement between your mother and Joe Watts?"

She got up and went to her bed. She lifted up the mattress and drew out a thin purse.

"Deputy let me bring this in the first night. We stopped past the apartment to get it." She dug in it and extracted a document which she handed me. There were several pages to it and it was one of the carbon copies, but it was signed by Alma Moffat and Joseph G. Watts.

I looked it over with some care while she watched and waited, fidgeting a little.

The agreement was not particularly complicated. Most of its length was given over to listing the various properties owned by Joe Watts, plus estimating those properties' values. The value of the land was given at just over one million dollars. Total value for all properties was a little below four million for Watts. There was also a listing, much smaller, but still impressive, for Mary Ann's dead mother.

"How did you get this?" I asked.

"Mother gave it to me a few weeks before she was killed."

"Who has the original copy?"

She shook her head. "I don't know. I don't ever remember seeing any other copy than this."

"But you got this one out of the apartment you sometimes shared with your mother the night that you shot at Joe Watts?"

"Yes. Is it important?"

"Maybe. Let me ask you about something else. After you

left Joe Watts's house did he ever try to get you to move back?"

"Yes." She thought for a moment. "No, not exactly. He called me a lot and asked me to go to dinner with him or to just talk to him, but I don't think he ever did ask me to move back in his house."

"All right. And when you were in the house living with Watts and your mother was there any area of the house you weren't allowed to enter?"

She gave me a peculiar look. "Who told you about that?"

"Believe I'm psychic. Was there?"

She nodded. "There was a workshop on the first floor. No one was allowed in it. A big room at the back of the house with no windows and only one door. A steel door. He kept it locked." She shrugged. "Once he let people in it, because I've been in it. But when I moved out that last time he told me he was working on something in that room, that what he was working on could be dangerous, and that no one was allowed in that room. I thought maybe it was something on automobiles."

I nodded. I leaned back and read the agreement again, skipping the parts that listed the items of property. The contract provided that the properties of the parties remain their separate properties, but it further provided that Alma, if she remained married to Joe Watts for more than three years, would receive two hundred thousand dollars a married year from his estate if he predeceased her or the same amount per year upon the dissolution of the marriage.

I finished and put the contract in my inner pocket and sat there thinking.

"How long were your mother and Joe Watts married?"

"Almost four years."

"Six hundred thousand dollars," I said. "He couldn't afford for her to be alive. At least that's how I'm going to paint it in court."

"But she's dead," she said.

I nodded. "I want a key to your apartment."

She got the purse again and took one out. She smiled at me.

"I'd rather give you this when I'm out of here." She reddened at her own brave joke.

I put the key in my pocket.

"Do you need more money yet?"

I was tempted, but I shook my head. "Not yet." I kept thinking about all that other money.

"Has Joe Watts suffered any financial reverses recently?"

"I don't know, Don. I want to help, but I don't know. He used to get that financial paper from Wall Street and read it for hours and I know he bought and sold some stocks, but I don't know whether he made or lost money. There always seemed to be plenty."

"I've heard he fired some of his help out there and that he drinks second-rate whiskey," I said.

She shrugged. "I still don't know."

"Was your mother a good driver?"

"No. She had her insurance canceled once. But she wasn't driving that day when he killed her." She looked away and then back.

"Was she the kind who'd be apt to wear her seat belt?"

"Sometimes maybe. Sometimes not."

"Did she put it on usually when she rode with Watts?"

"I just don't remember. She wasn't much for them. Once she unhooked the wires that buzz the little buzzer when you don't buckle up. And she wouldn't drive the kind that make you buckle up before the motor will start."

"So it would have been very probable that she could have been in Watts's car and not buckled in when he was in his seat belt?"

She nodded reluctantly.

I got up. I felt for my inside pocket. The agreement between Joe Watts and his deceased wife was there.

"Do you have to go?" she asked. She leaned her head toward me so that her eyes were shadowed and I couldn't see them.

"Yes. I want to go past your apartment."

"It gets lonely here."

She kissed me before I got to the cell door.

She said: "Please. Please get me out of here. If I killed that man I didn't mean to do it. I swear it. I've got to get out of here."

"I know." We nodded solemnly at each other.

The smiling deputy let me out and I wondered if he'd eavesdropped on us, seen me kissing her. Maybe I was just getting psychotic. That was highly possible.

I got the Plymouth and drove to Mary Ann's apartment building. I was impressed. It stood on half a block of ground, a two-story brick building, well kept, nicely landscaped. In the main hall I counted the mailboxes. There were twenty of them including Mary Ann's.

Her door opened to the key.

The rugs were very thick and soft. A light turned on noiselessly at my touch revealing a small kitchen beside me. It opened all along its far wall to a large living room. Doors led from the living room to two bedrooms. Each bedroom had an individual bath.

I opened closets and checked drawers. I couldn't tell whether anyone had been here before me or not, whether there'd been other searchers.

It was the kind of apartment that rents for much money.

I had a vague feeling of letdown as I prowled it. In the jail Mary Ann was mine. I was the master of her fate. If she got back out here she was her own woman again.

And yet that was what I was being paid for.

I turned off the lights and locked the door and went home and to bed. All night, in my dreams, I kept repeating that kiss. I'd half wake up, realize it was a dream and that the dream was pleasanter than reality, and so slide back down into it, smiling maybe. I was awake twice before I realized that vaguely, in the dreams, Joe Watts was still watching us/me. That ended the smiling.

I got up early, still tired, but glad the night was done. I had a shave and shower and then breakfast. When it was late enough I called Virginia and told her I wouldn't be in until afternoon.

At the edge of town I got on the interstate. I drove it carefully. It was foggy and the cars that were out this early were running in scared coveys with lights on. I joined one.

The road ran north and then surrendered to two lanes near the county line. At certain times of the year that two-lane stretch was a real bottleneck, but it wasn't anything to worry about on this day. The Florida traffic, north- and southbound, was gas-slack for now and most of the travelers were probably businessmen on their way to early appointments or truck drivers trying to make Indianapolis by noon.

I exited just south of the county line road, a mile before the four lane petered out. I proceeded west on a well-maintained road. For a time there was no other traffic on the road. It was the kind of rural road normally constructed of dirt and stone, but this road was wide and smooth and thickly asphalted. A Joe Watts road.

I thought I knew pretty well where Watts's land lay, but I got my copy of the accident report out and pulled off on the berm and studied it again. I was on the right road, but hadn't driven far enough yet.

As I sat there I saw a car approach from the other direction. It was a Cadillac Eldorado, black on black, ten or eleven thousand dollars' worth of automobile. I watched it go by with admiration. Two men were in the front seat. The license plate showed the car was from an adjoining state. I wrote the number down on the edge of the accident report. I figured the car must have come from the Watts place.

I drove on. In half a mile I ran into a long, silver metal fence, freshly painted, very high, with barbed wire in a "V" at the top of the barrier. It was the sort of fence you might see around a professional athletic field or a prison, difficult to go over without planned effort. And hadn't Mary Ann said it was electrified?

The road curved a bit and I slowed, realizing I'd found the location of the fatal accident. I stopped and pulled my Plymouth to the edge of the road and looked around carefully. On my right, a hundred feet or so up the road, there was a huge double metal gate, now closed. A tank would have had problems with it. As I watched a German shepherd dog crossed the road behind the gate, caught my scent and stopped to watch me suspiciously, then finally continued on into the heavy undergrowth at the far side of the road inside the fence. On back that inner road, visible through the baby-leafed trees, I could see a house. It was a huge house, all in brick and limestone, with pillars that supported a three-story-high porch in front. Some kind of construction was going on near it, intense and busy. I saw three snorting bulldozers pushing earth, red earth, similar to the color of earth I'd seen before. I thought I counted at least a dozen men working here and there.

When I tired of watching the construction I inspected the other side of the country road, looking away from Watts land. There the terrain was hilly and wild. I knew who owned that land, or thought I did. There was a kind of commune back there maybe a quarter of a mile distant. The commune was peopled by gentle kids, mostly college drop-outs from the state university in Bington, children too weak or weary or too hung out to journey on further to whatever was to be the next step. Once, I'd represented successfully three of them who'd been collectively arrested for vagrancy and another time I'd drawn a contract for the commune and a local merchant on leather goods they made.

The stump was on the commune's side of the road. I walked on over and examined it. When I drew near I could see the signs of damage on the stump, deep scars in the wood, still fairly fresh. The stump was about four feet high and I debated with myself for a moment about that, trying to figure why a woodsman would cut it off that high. Maybe it had been hit by lightning and sawed where convenient. Maybe it had been cut high as a boundary marker of some kind. Maybe the wood below the cut line was not usable. I shrugged. Anything was possible.

Watts had driven hard down his road, I supposed, and accelerated after leaving the double gate. He'd entered the curve too fast and skidded into the stump. He'd been lucky and she'd been unlucky. It happens.

The whole thing made me feel spooky. I felt like I was not only intruding, but being caught at it. I turned toward the big house again and watched. In a few seconds I was rewarded by a flash of light, sun reflecting from glass. Someone was watching me from atop that three-story-high porch. By straining my eyes I could make out a man up there watching me through glasses. The way the watcher moved made me certain it was Alvin Suedell.

Seeing him up there reminded me I'd talked to him about Mary Ann's case when I'd first gotten into it. I hadn't seen him since, except for his days in court when I'd sought bond for Mary Ann.

I looked again. It was Alvin. I was sure of that.

World's greatest card player . . .

I went back to the car and leaned against it, remembering.

Of all the people who are actively involved in the workings of the "other party" in Bington and Mojeff County, I know Alvin Suedell best. He's a kind of a friend, although he handles me gingerly, trusts me not at all, and only uses me in non-political work. But I have advised him at times and once even represented him in a piddling law suit which we piddled to a successful conclusion.

Alvin's a happily married man according to his wife. She ignores his bad habits and he pays her bills. I believe Esther, his wife, probably leached the best of his juices out years ago anyway and now he operates on instinct and memory, very carefully. I don't think Esther thinks about him much, just lets him move around easily as long as it costs nothing. She has her Lincoln and she can put away a lot of booze at her card parties at the Elks and country club. Maybe she believes that in return for that Alvin should have a little fun.

He does.

But I like him and he likes me and when I'd taken Mary Ann's case he'd seemed like a likely place to start, to try to figure what was happening.

That first day, after I'd heard Mary Ann's story in her cell, I'd known where I'd most likely find Alvin, for in the back room of the downtown Moose Club, back of the bar, there's a secluded room where one can find a bit of the sporting blood of Bington. It's a card room filled with round and square tables, hard chairs, and quiet waitresses who appear only on call and who scurry out after delivering their orders.

Alvin's an inveterate gambler, one of those men who are most happy with cards in hand.

I used my key in the club door. The barroom, which I entered first, had only a sparse crowd of work escapees and late lunchers at this time of day. I decided against a drink and went back through the swinging doors into the card room. The floor was carpeted and on the walls there were pictures of past Kentucky Derby winners and framed royal flushes held by members.

Smoke hung in the room like autumn haze. There were two rum games going, four players in each game, seated around square tables, intent upon the cards, cursing or smiling or stolid faced. No one looked up at me. Each man was in his private world.

In the back of the room was the big game. Around a fancy poker table ten men sat. The game was five card stud poker, one down, four up. The game had never varied since I'd been in Bington. Straight poker, no wild cards. The limit was ten dollars, the ante a dollar, three raises. An unwritten rule was that if you couldn't afford to play you didn't play. Some men I knew were forever barred for one reason or another.

I knew also that reputations had been made and lost at the table.

Alvin Suedell sat in his chair and looked curiously at the hole card he held. He saw me, but declined to speak. I stood and waited the hand out. On the last card he caught a king to an open king, bet the limit, and raked in the pot when no one called.

It improved his temper a bit. He winked at me.

"Something I can do for you, Robak?"

"When you want to take a little break I'd like to talk to you."

He debated with himself and curiosity won out. "Wait this game through. I need to see if I'm hot-hot or if that last hand was a fluke."

I nodded and waited. After two cards were turned a smiling man on the far side of the table made open aces and Alvin folded his hand.

"Deal me out for a few games," he said. He looked over at the smiling winner. "Don't die," he said.

He took my arm in friendly fashion and led me out the swinging doors and into the bar. We found a secluded, dark corner and sat down.

"Want a drink?" he asked solicitously.

"No, thanks."

He nodded approvingly. "Bad to drink at this time of day. Kill a young man like you. Now, what's on your mind?"

"State's listed you as a witness in the Tuttle mess," I said. "My client said maybe I might talk to you. I wanted to go over things with you before the bond hearing."

He shook his head dolefully. "You oughtn't to be in this one, Don. I'm for sure telling you that. She come out on Mr. Watts's place and took a shot at him. Then when we tried for the gun she shot poor old Roger. Mr. Watts is unhappy. He don't like notoriety like that. And when Mr. Watts is unhappy usually someone pays for it."

"Someone must defend her."

"Sure," he said. "But that don't mean it ought to be you. Word's around you could be someone in your party if ever you'd want to be, maybe run for a state office. They like you up there around the statehouse. But you mess around with Mr. Watts and you'll wind up with crap all over you." He gave me a long, knowing look. "Let her get someone else."

I was tempted. She was a pretty girl and she had enough money to pay my fee, yet I was tempted. And I was a little ashamed at the temptation. The thing was that I knew myself, knew I really wasn't a battler, only a plugger with a medium temper and a gift for words.

I said: "She's tried to hire several other people, but she hasn't been able to get anyone to take it. She thinks that's because Mr. Watts has put the word out."

His voice got a little harder. "Maybe he has."

I gave him my best innocuous grin. "I guess that leaves me."

"But why?"

I thought about it, willing to be reasonable in an unreasonable world. "She's got some money and can pay me. And I don't owe Watts a thing. Plus she has to have a lawyer."

He looked me over glumly. "Then I don't think I ought to talk to you."

"How come?"

"Watts wouldn't like it."

"All I want to know is what happened from an eyewitness. Maybe if I learn that I can maybe deal the whole thing with the prosecutor's office."

He hesitated and then nodded. "She hid out in some bushes up near the house. She was mad at Mr. Watts. Maybe she's nuts or something. I don't know. She's been running around claiming Watts killed her mother. Crazy. Crazy. She was out there when we come out of the house. There were the four of us."

"Who?" I asked.

"Mr. Watts, Polly, Roger, and me," he said without hesitation. "She took a shot at us and I heard the slug whistle right past my ear. Scared the crap right out of me, but Roger took a run at her and so I followed him. Polly was with us, too. We tried to get the gun away from her peaceable. Somehow she got it pointed at Roger and pulled the trigger."

"Was she trying to shoot Roger or did the gun just go off during the struggle?"

"She had it pointed. She was so damned mad she was almost frothing at the mouth. Calling names and things out that I wouldn't have thought she'd have known. The gun went off and Roger fell. I think Polly clipped her about the time of the shot. She went down, too. Roger got hit in the chest. Bad luck, I guess. The doc said he was dead in a matter of seconds. She was still out when the ambulance came. I never heard about her being sorry, if she is." He sneered and shook his head. "The town out there don't like it much, Don, but I could care less. Roger wasn't much. She's a big, good-looking broad. Maybe you can do her some good. But you get a bunch of money from her, because Watts ain't going to like you one bit and he fights hard."

I nodded.

He grinned and looked back at the doors of the card room.

"I got to get back. I'm due out at Watts's farm in a little bit and I want to get a few more games in."

"You staying out there?" I asked.

"Not exactly," he said. "Today I've got the word to give him about Mary Ann having a lawyer." He smiled without humor.

I nodded and let him go.

Now, I bent and examined the tree stump and the damage upon it carefully, moved slowly around it, then stopped and examined it from yet another angle. If I was being watched it seemed the right thing to do. When I'd done that for a while I walked up even with the gate, counting my steps. It was a distance of thirty-nine steps, probably closer to a hundred and ten feet than a hundred. I nodded my head for Alvin, still assuming it was him, then walked back. I opened the door of the Plymouth and sat there for a moment, then got out quickly, trying to register excitement, and looked the stump over again, all the time aware of the watcher, playing out my little scene for his benefit.

I figured he'd had plenty of time to grow curious about my behavior so I got back into the Plymouth, started up, and drove back toward the interstate road. I kept steady watch in my mirror and was soon rewarded. In a bit I saw a car coming quickly up behind me. I took the accident report out of my inner pocket and shoved it down into the seat. I added the contract between Watts and Mary Ann's mother and the two reports from the coroner. There was plenty of room under the loose padding.

The car coming up behind was the yellow Rolls-Royce. It stayed behind me for a time and then it proceeded around me at high speed. The driver then reduced speed, so that I was forced to cut my own speed sharply. I saw that Polly was driving. He turned and smiled back at me. There was someone in the back seat, but I couldn't make out who it was. I thought it might be county chairman Alvin Suedell, but maybe it was Joe Watts himself.

We were still about a mile from the interstate. All of this attention, even if I'd invited it, was making me nervous. I could feel a few drops of perspiration run down my back, although the day wasn't that warm. I reached over and locked the far door of the Plymouth and then the door beside me. I rolled the partly open driver's window almost to full closed. It squeaked in protest. I tightened my defective seat belt, making certain I didn't touch it below the buckle and snap it open.

They'd falsely reported I'd attacked Joe Watts and I'd decided if they'd do that then they probably would also falsely report the facts surrounding a death—maybe two deaths. I didn't know what they had in mind for me, but I made myself a quick promise that if they were going to stop me for more than discussion they were going to have to peel me out of the Plymouth before beginning the job.

At a small bridge Polly pulled the Rolls crosswise in the road, partially blocking it. I stopped ten yards away and turned off the motor.

The rear door of the Rolls opened and a smiling Joe Watts alighted. He came toward my car. I smiled back at him.

"I wanted to talk to you," he said, when he was near enough. "Sue said you were a reasonable man and so did my sheriff. Maybe we can do some business and stop our troubles."

"Maybe," I said. "Why now? You'll be seeing me in court on several matters soon enough. Why chase me down on a country road?"

He continued to smile. "I just wanted to see what could be arranged."

"What did you have in mind?"

"Maybe my stepdaughter could get other counsel and you could withdraw. Then, if you'd sign something for me promising not to sue, I could dismiss the affidavit I've filed against you."

I looked him over. He was impeccably dressed in a bright blue and white suit, all small checks. He had on dark shoes, a white shirt, and a splendid tie.

"How about her?" I asked.

"Nothing will happen to her," he said. He smiled even more, revealing expensive bridgework. "I don't want much to happen to her." He nodded. "I like her, you know. I'll make certain not much happens to her. I've a lot of friends. I guess you've found that out."

"You tell me exactly what you're going to do and how you expect to accomplish it and if it suits her I might withdraw," I said.

"I'm not giving you any details," he said with his first show of annoyance. "It'll work out my way no matter what you do. I just dislike the idea of you running around here and there checking on me. I want it stopped. It's embarrassing."

"I find it illuminating," I said.

His face grew darker. "Look at you," he said with contempt. "You drive this old rattletrap and my friends tell me you're perpetually short of money." He waited.

"I'm not for sale, Mr. Watts."

"Horse crap," he said.

"Make me a specific offer about her, Mr. Watts," I encouraged.

He shook his head. "For now any thought of an offer is

withdrawn. When you've had some time to think things over then you can call me." He nodded a little and turned away and said back over his shoulder: "I believe I'll let Polly reason with you now."

"I'm not trying to be unreasonable," I said. "I only want a few assurances . . ."

He didn't stop or say anything more to me. He moved to his Rolls, back rigid. He opened the driver's door and Polly got out. A few low words were passed and they exchanged positions. Polly walked up close and he smiled at me also. His look was almost apologetic. He was wearing a sweatshirt and ragged pants. There were traces of red clay on his shoes. That angered me.

"Mr. Watts, he wanted me to talk to you about a few things, Don." He leaned forward confidentially. "I'm sorry. I got to do this."

"Get the car out of my road, Polly," I said. I pushed the Plymouth's starter button and the motor chugged into reluctant life.

"I want you to get out now so we can talk about things," he lied, yelling a little so I could hear him over the sound of the motor.

"Why not drop into the office again? This time for a talk," I said.

He ignored my answer and moved up very close to the Plymouth. He wasn't as tall as I thought he was, but he seemed about a yard wide at the shoulders. I remembered the scared kid he'd once been. Now he looked like the "after" part of the ad you see now and then in the men's magazines where they're trying to sell you a body-building course.

I knew he was plus thirty years old, around my age. He was starting to go bald in front.

He whined: "Get out, Don. Don't make this any harder for me." His eyes pleaded with me and his movements were jerky and nervous.

I grinned at him. The grin was the product of my own nerves. He put another kind of meaning to the grin and he shook his head.

"That was private property back there you was trespassing on," he said.

"The road, too?" I asked carefully, seeing that he was trying to work himself up to anger. "My map shows it's a county road."

"Sue told Mr. Watts you got over on his property when you was out of your car. Mr. Watts told me I was to make you remember not to do that again."

"I'll remember," I said.

"No. Not that easy. You step out and I'll make sure you remember." He called me a string of dirty, interesting names, some of which I was guilty of. I assumed the names were meant to bring me screaming in rage out of the car. I waited until he was finished.

"If you're all done I guess I'll stay in here," I said politely. "If you've delivered your message you tell Mr. Watts I think he's a fine fellow also."

He nodded angrily and took a handkerchief out of his pocket and wrapped it around his hand. I watched, fascinated. He cursed for effect and strength and hit the window beside me with a short, pumping stroke. It was a hard smash and it starred the window, but opened no hole. The handkerchief slipped a bit and he readjusted it with his free hand, making ready again.

I said: "I'm going to get you, Polly."

His eyes flickered with surprise. Even after all the long

years he wasn't sure. His childhood reflexes remained. He stopped and thought about it.

I backed the Plymouth away carefully while he stood there. Maybe he knew there was no place for me to go of value. I could go back toward Watts's place, but that didn't seem like much of a chance to him. He adjusted the handkerchief and, when I stopped, he walked toward me.

I had enough room for a good run. I put the Plymouth in low and drove forward and butted him pretty hard with the left front fender. He'd stopped and begun to move the other way when I got up to him, maybe not really believing I'd hit him. When I did hit him the force of the blow knocked him rolling into the ditch that had necessitated the bridge. He stayed there, watching, making no attempt to come up and out.

I drove onto the bridge. The yellow Rolls hadn't moved. Watts watched me clinically from behind the wheel. I saw him reach over and lock his doors.

I aimed for the shiny side panel of the Rolls and drove into it at slightly in excess of five miles an hour. There was a very satisfactory banging, metal-tearing sound. Joe Watts looked out at me in disbelief. He leaned forward and yelled something at either me or at Polly, still in the ditch. I couldn't hear what it was he yelled.

I put my foot to the accelerator and pushed down, remembering what our office had looked like. Both cars moved a little, the Rolls sliding sideways a trifle and the Plymouth crumpling its way into the new area that lay vacant. There still wasn't room to drive through so I pushed harder on the accelerator. Tires screamed and I thought the Plymouth was going to quit, the motor burn up, the clutch slip.

Watts made a frantic motion, shaking his head. He started

the Rolls. He pulled the yellow car, now bearing side lacerations, out of my way.

I was sweating and frightened. I drove away recklessly. In my rear-view mirror I could see Polly arising now from the haven he'd found in the ditch, brushing at himself. His face was contorted and I thought he might be crying. I fancied he also had a limp.

I drove on back and entered the interstate road. Once there I pulled over to the berm, where a sign warned EMERGENCY STOPPING ONLY. I sat there for a time shaking, my imagination writing other endings for the scene in which I'd just performed. From where I stopped I could see far down Watts's road. No yellow car followed me and I wondered thankfully why.

I drove back to town after examining the car. The right front fender was pushed in and one headlight was knocked out and there were new bumps and abrasions on the front and side where there hadn't been bumps and abrasions before. Plus the fact that the driver's side window was starred.

It appeared to be the season for caution. I drove to the police station and made out an "accident" report with the help of the patrolman who had desk duty. I made the report out in duplicate. I had him sign my carbon copy and time stamp it. My state has a law that directs you to report all "accidents" within forty-eight hours where no peace or police officer is called to the scene.

Handy wandered in when we were finishing. I solemnly repeated the story to him, minimizing it where I could. He grinned and followed me out to inspect the Plymouth.

He touched the streaks of yellow paint on the fender.

"One thing," he said. "Did you put down on the accident

report that your vehicle was damaged totally or did you put down five dollars?"

I patted the Plymouth on her battered hood and said to it and Handy: "She's a winner."

He shook his head. "I'd hate to see a loser."

"Are you going to check my story?"

"Not us, baby," he said with perfect equanimity. "We check accidents for the sheriff when he asks us, but nothing else in the county. If you want me to make a copy of your report and send it on to him I'll do that."

I thought for a moment. It didn't seem like the best of ideas. The only reason I was filing the report was to forestall any further criminal actions on Watts's part.

I said: "Forget it." I got out my billfold, found the slip, and handed it to him. "Can you find out who owns a Cadillac Eldorado with this license number?"

He took it from me and nodded.

"You find anything along the fingerprint line in the office?"

He shook his head. "No. My boys think whoever it was wore gloves, but it was a cold night that night." He gave me a hard look. "You keep on messing around and messing around," he said. "Things will pop. Maybe you'll pop with them." He shook his head. "Word's out on you. Prosecutor says you don't get the right time of day."

"Is it right for him to say that, Handy?"

He waited, saying nothing.

"Or, more than that, for someone else to tell him he has to say it?" I asked.

"What am I supposed to do?" he asked.

I smiled, although nothing was funny. "Maybe stay with me when I'm right and be against me when I'm wrong."

He nodded. "I didn't make the world, Don." He put the

license number in his billfold, not meeting my eyes. "I'll find out whose number this is."

"Thanks," I said.

———◆———

Quinn's Body Shop was located east of town several miles up the river road. I drove there past houses that had endured decades of seasonal floods and been damaged, but not destroyed. Here and there new places had been built in the flood plain, most of them raised high on stilts. A few fishermen sat along the banks of the river or fished out of small boats near the shore. Everywhere there were new boats, old boats, and the rotting hulks of dead boats.

Quinn's had a high metal fence which was covered with vines to semi-hide the wrecks behind, but a glance told the observer that this was an automobile burial ground.

I parked and locked the Plymouth, figuring that otherwise some diligent employee might take it for a new arrival and cannibalize it.

The main building was long and low, constructed of concrete blocks, and almost windowless. I entered. Here and there naked electric bulbs hung down, bright spots in the gloom. In one corner of the building a burly man used a welding torch on something. The near quarter of the building was partitioned off and a small metal sign on a door in the middle of the outer wall of the quarter said: OFFICE.

I tapped on the door and then went on in.

There was a high counter and several desks and filing cabinets. At one desk a thin girl pecked at a typewriter. She frowned at me when I came in.

"I'd like to see one of your cars," I said.

She got up and came to the counter. She had a bad, paralytic limp and when she drew close I saw she really wasn't a girl, but a woman, thirty to forty years old, with a thin, sparrow body and undefeated eyes.

"You from insurance?" she asked.

"Not exactly. I'm a lawyer. I wanted to look over the car Mrs. Watts was killed in."

She decided for me. "Okay," she said. "You come on with me and I'll show you." She reached under the counter and fumbled there. "You want pictures?"

I nodded. "It could help."

She brought out a camera that looked like a good one. "You tell me what you want and I'll shoot it. Buck and a half each, which includes the negative. If I have to testify that's extra."

I nodded and then followed where she led. She stopped near where the burly man was still using his welding torch on what I now recognized as an auto frame.

"You hear the telephone then catch it, Smitty."

He nodded somberly at her.

Outside the sun had vanished again. She led me down a row of wrecks and back a side row. In the distance I could see a heavy crane loading old auto bodies aboard a transport truck.

"It's here," she said and stopped.

There was room to walk all the way around it. I did so. Someone had already removed the wheels and some parts from the motor, plus the steering wheel and probably many things I failed to notice. On the driver's side the Fibreglas body was slightly buckled, but the frame seemed undamaged. The passenger side was the area of extensive damage. The car must have impacted the tree, after the skid, right in front of the juncture of the door with the front fender, and continued on back as the car had slid, so that all behind the door post and the front part of the door was wiped away and the passenger compartment was open to the elements back to where the rear bumper was bent away. The frame at the bottom was scarred and bent, but not too badly. I bent down and looked at the right front door post, which still remained attached to the hood and part of the roof. I thought there was a substance darker than rust on the door post and there was more of the same substance on the fractured windshield. I decided it was blood.

The girl waited patiently.

"Could I have some pictures of this area?" I asked.

She nodded and bent to the task.

I had her take pictures of the side of the car, the frame, and the seat area and then I had her take pictures of the other side of the car, where there was little damage. I could see myself having them marked for identification in a whispering courtroom, handing them to Watts, and asking him embarrassing questions.

When she'd finished the roll of film I bent down and looked around inside for the last time, but there wasn't anything, at least now. The glove compartment was empty and there was nothing under the seats.

"Okay," I said. "I've got enough."

She nodded and I followed her slow progress back to her office.

"I took a dozen shots," she said. "I'll make them to you for fifteen bucks. What say I develop them over the weekend and you pick them up first of the week?"

I nodded. "Fine."

"Funny you should come in right after that man called," she mused.

"How's that?"

"The man who used to own the car called this morning. He wanted to know if the car was still here."

I thought about that for a moment.

"I'll look for you then, Mr. . . . ?" She waited for the answer to her question.

"Robak," I said. "Donald Robak. I'm an attorney downtown. Adams and Robak."

If it meant anything to her she didn't give anything away.

"If that man or anyone else comes around I'd appreciate it if you say nothing about me being here. Maybe we could make it twenty-five for the pictures that way."

She nodded enthusiastically.

I unlocked the Plymouth, got in, and thought for a minute or two.

There was another place I'd thought about wanting to go, a man I knew I wanted to see.

I drove on out to the lake. Curt Markman lives in a cottage out there. I'd been there a few times for political and nonpolitical parties, but it had been a while. I'd heard a rumor, a few weeks back, that he'd had some hard luck.

The lake is private and fenced, but the college boys have been very democratic about using it, fence or no. It's common knowledge that most fraternity houses have a key to the gate lock, which is usually unlocked anyway.

Markman has a small cottage. He's one of the few permanent residents. He's a quiet man. I'd been his first, and now probably his only, representative in the state house. He's my county chairman.

He'd been happy at my election. He'd come visiting several times while the session was on and I'd escorted him out on the town, introduced him to names he'd only heard, and listened carefully to his advice. As a result he'd taken it far harder than I had when I'd lost out for re-election.

I hadn't seen him for a while because he'd been in and out of hospitals. I'd sent him cards and once I'd received a scrawled, cheerful note from him about "next election."

The gate was open. I could see him from the gravel road when I got near. He was sitting on his front porch rocking away in an ancient chair, well bundled against the still cool morning. He wore a heavy coat and a winter golf cap with pull-down earflaps, partially hiding his lank gray hair. His eyes, when I was near enough to see them, were about the same as I'd remembered them, thin blue in color, cynical, and somehow solitary without being lonely.

I parked the Plymouth in his pull-off area and walked on up to the porch.

He nodded to me. His voice was weak, but it had never been strong. He said: "Welcome to hard times." He grinned, taking any bitterness out of the statement.

I'd heard they'd found he had an inoperable cancer and I inspected him. He'd always been thin, but he seemed thinner now, but not by a lot. He also seemed bowed a little, as if someone had bent him in the middle. Otherwise he seemed what he'd always been. He reminded me a little of an old man I'd prepared a will for a few months back, a man who was mostly angry about what was happening, a man unready to admit final defeat, fighting from every hedgerow.

"I almost didn't recognize you without your fishing pole," I said.

He looked lake and sky over with practiced eyes. "Not today," he said. "No use." He turned back to me. "What are you doing out here in the daytime and without some girl in heat?" For some reason he'd always considered me to be something of a lover, although I'd done nothing I knew of to give him that impression.

I smiled. "I wanted to talk to you about Joe Watts."

"Him?" he questioned. "I heard you was in a pickle with him." He shook his head. "He can buy you long and sell you short, Don. Us little-potatoes politicians want to play it coy and careful when he's around. Suedell's a minor dreamer compared to Watts."

"Tell me some way to get a hold on him, Curt. Tell me anything you know."

He shook his head. "Ain't no way to get around all that money and cussedness. We're nothings to him. Even if you got something he knows too many up and down the ladder. Prosecutor would laugh at you." He grinned. "But and however . . ."

"Yes?"

"He came down here from Detroit. I talked to some people at a convention one time from up around there. I got told that he made it out of there about five steps ahead of a grand jury investigation. He was some kind of wheel up there with one of the auto companies. They said he was in charge of research and did testing. He had a lot of stock. They began having trouble with their new line which he'd tested and it seems it turned out that he'd sold all his stock and some more short just about a week before the trouble surfaced. Got bad enough that they suspended trading in the stock for a time. Some said he caused the problem, but he was out of the country for a time, and nothing ever happened." He leaned back in his chair and rocked it carefully.

"When was that?"

He rocked a little harder and the movement seemed to hurt him a little, but he kept on.

"Right before he came here," he said. He grinned again and it was an attractive grin, younger than the man, undaunted by trouble, unwilling to admit disaster.

"You know anyone up around Detroit?" he asked.

"No, but I've got a friend who does." I was thinking of Handy. Maybe he'd know something. I'd ask.

We talked a while longer about the party and its forbidding future in Mojeff County, but I saw he was tiring.

"I've got to go. I'll come back later."

"Soon," he said, smiling. "Come back soon, Don. Maybe to fish?"

I nodded.

When I drove away he was rocking in the old chair again, moving more gently now, watching the rippled surface of the lake.

Back in the office Virginia handed me a phone message. "Prosecutor keeps calling for you, but the Senator asked that you talk to him before you talk to the prosecutor."

"All right," I said. "Is the Senator alone?"

She nodded coldly. Her look implied that all this Humpty-Dumpty wasn't doing the Senator any good.

"Your boys did a good job getting the books back up and in order," I said lamely.

"Hmmph," she said.

I marched away and into the Senator's office. Things really did look good. It was the neatest his office had been in recent months.

He sat in his chair, contemplating that neatness with disbelief, looking old and tired. He said: "The prosecutor called me about the venue and jury trial motions I sent to city court. He didn't seem very happy. He wants you to come talk to him. I believe he wants to know what kind of a deal you'd make with him on a judge to hear your case down there."

"Well I'd accept any unbiased, unprejudiced judge that Watts can't get to. Does he have any around like that?"

The Senator shook his head. "I'd doubt it and you should be very damned careful about who you accept as a special judge. Watts does have a lot of people who are beholden to him in this town and those people can't automatically be picked out." He waited, letting me read nothing in his old eyes.

"Okay. We'll accept that. But I have to take a chance with someone. Try thinking of some names I might have a sporting chance with?"

"I thought you'd never ask," he said, nodding. "I'll point out you can get had by anyone, but I've done some thinking about who's least likely to get at you, and, if it were my rear end moving toward the saw, I'd get the three best I could think of on the panel. For three likely people I'd go with Judson Burke, Bill Dotcher, and maybe Henry Fanlein." He nodded again, this time to himself. "Then I'd hope I hadn't made a mistake and that everything went my way in the hearing. Also I'd pray a bunch."

"What if I had at least some evidence to show I wasn't and couldn't have been near Joe Watts that night?"

"You've got your evidence and they've got their evidence. Who's a judge supposed to believe?"

He was right about that, but I thought I had a good chance.

"I'll go face to face with Herman and maybe dig a little."

He nodded and went back to staring at his spic and span office, losing me. He'd worked a long time at getting his office into the sort of genteel untidiness that a good office has. Now he was going to have to start all over again. The prospect seemed to discourage him.

I walked down the steps and headed for the prosecutor's office. The sun was now out and I could smell the river a few blocks away, still in flood stage, but receding now. Soon it would be summer and the boaters would be here in Bington to squander their summer gas.

I considered Herman Leaks again, our new prosecuting attorney. He's the Jaguar driver and I've heard that his car cost about ten thousand dollars. I've also heard there's no lien on it, that it's his. He's now been prosecutor for a little over a year and his salary is fifteen thousand a year, plus some minor fringe benefits. I also know he was deep in debt when he was elected, but all is well now and he's had the Jag for seven or eight months.

Maybe it was a rich grandmother. *Bon* estate.

Herman's a mean, little man who quivers with nervous energy and who really doesn't like anyone. He's about forty years of age and he isn't married now. He goes with a lady who has some heavy old Bington money and they're supposed to be serious about it.

I'm sure he has visions of using his office and her money as stepping stones on his way upward toward the better land, which is part of the good old American dream.

Once, when he was in his cups and I was around, I heard Herman discussing Herman. Booze had loosened him up. He was living, that night, in the governor's chambers, sitting up there in that big, overgrown office, making earth-shaking decisions.

I know a lot of area lawyers who've pledged that it will never happen.

Herman is quite commonly known among his brothers at

the bar as "that bastard." When one rounds a corner in the courthouse and comes upon a whispered conversation and those two words are being used then the chances are 60/40 the conversation has to do with Herman. True, there are other bastards who practice in my vicinity and some judges who deserve the appellation, but most pale into insignificance when compared to Herman.

A prosecutor can be merciless and the bar will defend him if he's fair. A prosecutor can be soft and easy and lack ability and the bar will tuck into hiding his minor faults, speak well of him, and urge his re-election if he has the internal fortitude to run again.

But a lawyer must keep his word. Right or wrong, he must keep it. It is his holy of holies.

Herman's word has no value. He's slave to the last man who talks to him. He makes agreements, deals, plea bargains, and then backs away from them, twists out from under, reneges.

He has favorites, political cronies who cozy to him, use him. There are others that he chases after, ones he feels can help on the next step upward.

He is suspect to being for sale. Maybe not always openly for a certain sum of money, but a favor for a favor, a dismissal for the friend of a friend.

No harm in that.

Herman hates the job, despises most of the people he sees, fawns only after those who can help.

I remembered he'd dated Mary Ann's mother. Had that been before or after his affair with the lady with the Bington heavy money? It seemed to me that I recalled reading on the society page of the Bington *Chronicle* that the lady and Herman had announced their engagement or some such. Recently?

His office was in the courthouse. I was back in a waiting line. A uniformed officer winked at me. He was guarding a man in handcuffs. There were two ladies surrounded by five children—seekers of support. There was another lady with a black eye who undoubtedly wanted her husband and/or boy friend jailed for whacking her about.

I gave my name to a harassed secretary, who already knew me, but still expected me to give my name and wait, hat in hand. She vanished and returned in a bit, beckoning me out of turn while the crowd glared.

Herman sat behind his desk. He had some law books in front of him, but I figured they were more for show than for sure. He motioned me to a chair and I took it.

"Herman," I said, as if I was worried about the whole thing, "you called and wanted to see me?"

"Yes sir. That's sure right, Donny." He gave me a little smile and then laughed, all to show he was one good fellow.

He said: "I'm getting *mucho* pressure on this case that Joe Watts filed against you. I know you were up against him in court and it's okay with me that you were. But he says you come right out on his place and attacked him. And this office can't put up with that."

"Horse manure," I said.

"How's that?"

"Who's giving you the pressure? Citizen groups? The police? I'll bet the only pressure you're getting is from Watts himself."

He ignored that. "It isn't funny, Don. I've had some calls from the disciplinary committee wanting to know about the case and about you."

"I wonder just who got them interested in it before I was tried?" I asked.

He shook his head, without information he intended to divulge. "It's going to have to be tried, Don."

"Sure it is," I said. "There's also going to have to be a change of venue from the judge and maybe a trial by jury."

He grasped quickly at my choice of the word *maybe*. He's not completely stupid.

"If there has to be a trial by jury then we'll go ahead and file in circuit court."

"That's fine with me," I said. "I'm willing that it be filed there." I wasn't, but he didn't know that. I paused and then cast my line, its lure skimming over the water. "I suppose maybe we could try it in front of a judge alone in city court. But I'd have to name the panel and I'd want the striking process done now, without consulting with anyone about it. And I'd want a stenographer there to take down the evidence."

"Why a stenographer?"

"Part of what I want," I said stolidly. "And I won't agree to go ahead down there unless I get it." *If they told their lies on the witness stand then I wanted those lies down, word for word.*

He sat silently for a long moment and I thought he was going to refuse.

"If I agreed to those conditions then when could we try it?"

"Within reason I'll let you name the date. But all defenses must be open to me without special pleading, self defense, alibi—you know the routine. I'm not going to give up my jury and then be hurried and harried with a lot of Mickey Mouse."

"Could you try it this coming Monday?"

"Possibly," I said, sounding reluctant. "I'd want a list of your witnesses."

"They're all listed on the affidavit. There aren't any others."

"All right. That settles that."

I could almost hear the gears turning in his head. If he agreed to my deal he could call Boss Watts as soon as I left and crow loudly about how he'd brought me to my knees, forced me to trial, and so make some points. And yet he knew me. I'd boxed his ears and stolen his jockstrap before. He was leery of me.

"If I lose," I said, to give him some heart, "I'd certainly appreciate any help you can give me with the disciplinary people."

He laughed his useless laugh and decided he had me. I wondered how much he knew of what had happened. Did he know, for example, that I'd been in my apartment and could have no eyewitnesses to it, no one to help me? *It was possible.*

He said: "You know I'll be glad to do whatever I can." He refused to meet my eyes. "Give me the names of the panel?"

I gave them to him and he frowned, but we went ahead. I struck one name from the panel and he struck another and we were left with Judson Burke.

Judson's a man who has a fair local legal reputation and I wasn't unhappy with him as the selection. He drinks a bit, but it's hard to find anyone these days who's perfect—particularly in the mirror.

"Monday, then," he said.

I nodded.

"Uh—Don—I want you to know how sorry I am about all this. I wouldn't push at you if I wasn't being pushed."

"Sure," I said forgivingly.

He was encouraged and so traveled further. "Another thing, Don—the city judge don't like you taking changes of judge from him. He especially didn't like it in this case. He says it makes him look bad, like he wasn't fair or something."

"You apologize for me," I said, tongue in cheek. "Tell him with us being friends I didn't want to put him on the spot."

"I'll try to make it right with him," he said.

"Another thing," I said. "My client Mary Ann Moffat tells me you used to date her mother. Did you date her mother, Herman?"

There was a long moment of silence.

I said: "I'm going to have to know, Herman. If it becomes necessary I'll subpoena you to testify. I'll bring along some of the news media people when I issue you the subpoena. I don't want to be dirty, but I'm under a great deal of pressure myself in that matter." I gave him my finest sincere look.

"Just who told you about me going with Mrs. Watts?"

"About you going with her? It's sort of common knowledge. I can see how it could be embarrassing to you, what with maybe getting married and all, but the fact you once dated Mrs. Watts isn't much of a secret."

He gave me a distressed look. "We were only friends."

I shook my head. "That isn't the way I heard it." I made what I'd heard sound like a lot more.

"At first I didn't even know she was married to Joe Watts." He gave me a wounded look, perhaps remembering times I could only conjecture on. "As soon as I found out she was married to Joe it was strictly hands off."

"Where'd you meet her?"

"Walking. I take an evening walk. I swear I didn't know who she was."

"How long did you go with her? How many dates? How serious did things get?"

"She was only someone I knew," he said, shuddering. "And why pick on me? I'm not pushing the case against her daughter. I'll deal that one with you reasonably."

"What's reasonably?"

"How about you pleading her guilty to manslaughter?"

"Voluntary or involuntary?"

"Involuntary," he said.

"Would you recommend a suspended sentence?"

"No. She killed a man." His voice hardened.

"Maybe," I said. "One thing I know is that the same people who testified she killed Roger Tuttle in the bond hearing will be testifying against me."

He shrugged.

"She says she doesn't remember what happened," I said. "There was a fight for the gun. Four big men and one little girl. One of the men, a useless drunk by reputation, winds up dead and she's knocked unconscious."

"Try and sell what you can add together from that," he said, sneering.

"I will," I said confidently, as if I didn't have a care in the world. "I've got that and I'll have more after Monday. You tell them I know more than they think."

"I think she was maybe temporarily insane," he said. "When are you going to file your plea on that? That's your defense and you know it."

I smiled at him. "I'm not ready yet."

"We know what you're trying to do," he said, "and it won't work either."

"Who knows?" I said. "But back to the business at hand. I'd like for us to call Judson Burke while I'm here. That way there can't be any mistake, any misunderstanding. We can make sure he'll be the judge and that all the ground rules have been explained to him."

He nodded reluctantly.

I was allowed to listen in on the secretary's extension. Herman's waiting line watched me. I winked at the girl with the black eye, but she'd given up men for a while and took it without a smile.

Burke heard us out and then said: "I'll judge the case. It isn't much my kind of thing, but I'll judge it for you."

I wasn't sure whether I detected bourbon or disapproval in his voice. Nice lawyers don't have to defend themselves because they never get accused of bopping private citizens in the beak. Nice lawyers represent corporate clients, close mortgages, and belong to the Country Club and the Lions. Nice lawyers die rich, with leathery livers, and bored.

I had some second thoughts about Judson. We've known each other for some years without admiration. I shoved that problem back in my mind. The Senator had recommended him.

It had been polite of him to accept the case, but things deteriorate for the polite.

I remembered that I'd heard that in Capitol City, our lovely state seat, that half the bar now goes armed. It wasn't that bad in Bington—yet—and it would never be that bad for Judson. The normal lawyer sees the troubles of his town, hears its lies, is privy to the hidden secrets, and party to the lancing of the found abscesses. The thing was that Judson had removed himself from that arena because he'd grown wealthy. Now, when we asked him to notice part of it, he was disdainful, but polite.

Maybe I ought to tell him about Capitol City, but I decided he wouldn't believe it anyway.

I left the prosecutor's office without exchanging further words with Herman Leaks. The gage had been thrown, the lines drawn, the arena engaged. Monday.

I walked on over to the courthouse. I'd missed lunch, but you can't win them all.

There was an oversized map of the county in the auditor's office, dividing it into townships, further dividing the townships by sections. I examined the northern area until I picked out what I thought was the approximate location of Joe Watts's land. I got out the transfer books appertaining thereto and leafed through the pages, counting the various tracts owned in the name of Watts and also those in the name of J.G.W., Inc., a name that kept recurring and which I quickly surmised also covered Watts's property. Added up, unless I'd missed a few, there were more than thirty different tracts, split about half and half between individual ownership and corporate ownership. The various tracts fit together like some child's puzzle and totaled in excess of two thousand acres. A lot of land. There might be even more, land purchased on sale contract, but not yet deeded, in which he had equitable ownership.

I hefted the plat book into its rack and sat there thinking for a while. On a sudden impulse I went to the office of the Recorder and got out the books there. Every tract seemed to have been transferred to something called "Bington Home Developers, Inc.," by recent deeds. The transfers had been made two days before the death of Alma Watts. Possession was to be given ninety days from the date of the deeds, a time soon approaching. The deeds had been made by an old Bington law firm which I knew was above reproach. Alma Watts had signed the deeds as secretary of J.G.W., Inc. and for herself. Everything seemed to have been properly done.

And two days later she was dead.

Later, I took the courthouse elevator up to the fourth floor, skirted a few loungers who waited on the benches outside the courtroom, avoided a solitary spittoon, and found Judge Steinmetz in his office.

He was pawing through a mound of papers on his desk, seeking something. They drown judges in papers these days. He scratched his bald head, saw me in the midst of the scratching movement, and motioned me in. Frieda, his peerless court reporter, had vanished somewhere for the moment. I figured she was probably enjoying herself in the perpetual talkathon coffee mess in the clerk's office.

I sat down and waited and, in a while, he tired of looking. He said wryly: "Frieda probably hid it. She does that to make herself indispensable." He gave me an inquiring look.

"Can you be around and available on Monday?"

He frowned. "I can if necessary. I'm supposed to be elsewhere, but it's no emergency."

"I might want to call you as a witness in city court."

He watched me with slightly slanted eyes that had witnessed every excuse known to the race of men, but eyes which were still curious about this year's variations.

"What are you into now, Robak?" he asked me in his courteous voice.

"I find I'm accused of crime. It's alleged that I assaulted and battered a prominent, local citizen a few nights back."

"Joe Watts," he said. He reached over on his desk and

handed me a bedraggled copy of the Bington *Chronicle*. "There's a story on the back page in the city court news."

"So I heard. I am, of course, as pure as the first snow of winter."

He smiled at me. "Nevertheless you shouldn't have done it. It's illegal. Were there other witnesses?"

"Yes. Two other witnesses. Both gentlemen who work closely with Mr. Watts."

He nodded, knowing I'd get at *why* I needed him in my own sweet time. He changed the subject a bit: "I had some calls before and during the bond hearing on your pretty client. I am, as you may know, up for re-election next year, with primary time coming in less than a year." He stretched and scratched at his head again. "I sometimes am irritated when callers try to blend too many things into their conversations. In your Moffat case the blending was great interest in the possible outcome and a desire to know if I planned on running again."

"And what did you say about running again?" I asked curiously.

"I'm not much interested, Don," he said. "I've been on the bench for twenty-two years. I'm old enough to draw full retirement if I want. I can golf, mess around, golf, do a little estate work, and golf. I could probably survive without the pension off the quarters I could win from you on the golf course." He nodded, losing me, momentarily pleased with his own thoughts about happy days to come. "I pointed this out to the most insistent and important of my callers. He or she seemed unhappy about it. There was no further conversation and no information was passed on about your client. But suddenly, about that time, there were rumblings about a change of judge by the state. I noted to Mr. Leaks that if such a motion was filed I might feel compelled to admit Miss Moffat to bond before granting such a change."

"Thanks for that," I said. "Even if it didn't work out for her bond I know the extent of the case against her."

"I want to emphasize that the caller wasn't Joe Watts," he said. "The last caller was a person high in the ranks of my party, one of our numerous fixers, a man who seemed to think I owed him something. He won't again." He grinned at me.

I waited.

"It isn't any of your business who it was." He kicked his feet up on his desk and peered out his grimy window at the streets of Bington, four floors down. He seemed to forget I was there for a moment.

I spent the free time looking around his office, which always fascinates me. The walls are decorated, over every square inch, with the pictures of those who were now or had been his friends. One had later been President, several had been senators, and many of the others were familiar faces in the present arena of state politics. There's even the picture of one great man who's been convicted of bribery and done time in a federal penitentiary. I thought it showed something about the judge that he'd never removed that bad apple picture.

The judge has been asked, on at least several occasions, to run for the state supreme court. He's also been offered a federal judgeship.

But he's stayed in Bington.

He's the possessor of a memory like none I've ever seen or heard of. He can quote you pretty much word for word from ten thousand cases. The days of his life are separate pages to him, so that each day is single, and not to be confused with other days. I've heard him many times, in his careful, courteous voice, set someone straight about what weather conditions had been or what had happened on a certain argued date months or years back. I've never known him to be wrong.

It's a fearful gift. Judge Steinmetz remembered his griefs too well. There was no casual forgetfulness for him. And, from the occasional late night calls, I knew he was sorely wounded by his lack of ability to forget. He could temporarily blank memory by heavy drinking, but that brings other problems. Specifically, he suffers from ulcers and must drink sparingly at best. Sometimes, when it gets to be too heavy a load, I've seen him stun the ulcers with rapid icy martinis and away he goes.

He survives.

He turned back to me.

"I think the prosecution is aware how you and the Senator plan to bushwhack them."

I shrugged. Figuring it out meant little.

He said: "When I appoint my court psychiatrists you're not going to let them examine her. Or at least she won't help with the examination."

"That sounds like a good idea," I said, smiling. "I'm glad you suggested it."

He whinnied laughter.

"Just exactly when are you supposed to have assaulted Joe Watts?"

I told him.

———◆———

That evening I had the Bumstead cheeseburger-through-the-garden at a drive-in place near the university. Around me, as I ate it, college kids talked loudly, visiting cheerily from car to car as early moths buzzed about their neon forest.

I drove again to the jail. It was becoming a nightly habit, one I found difficult to break.

At the jail the cooks had fixed something that smelled like onions. The odor was strong enough to blank out the other smells of the jail.

She wouldn't look at me when the deputy took me in and opened her cell door. She let me come on into the inner cell and she sat down on the bed, her eyes downcast.

"What's wrong?" I asked.

She looked up at me and shook her head.

"Tell me what it is," I insisted.

"What have I gotten you into?" She looked away. When she said something again her voice was very low so that I had to concentrate to hear it.

"He came to see me today."

"Watts?"

She nodded.

"I hope you didn't say anything to him," I said carefully. "Was anyone with him?"

"No. Just him." Her face was agonized. "He said he had you in bad trouble. He wouldn't tell me what it was, but he said you could tell me about it if you wanted." She leaned toward me. "What is it, Don?"

"He got the prosecutor to accept an affidavit against me for assault. He thinks he has me cold. There's to be a trial in city court on Monday."

She shook her head, pained by what I was saying.

"Maybe the same thing he did to you. His witnesses, his place. I wasn't even there. I was in my own apartment. I don't want you to worry about it. If he comes again just don't talk to him at all."

"He doesn't like me hiring you, Don. He told me to get

rid of you and my troubles would vanish. He's angry at you instead of me." She shook her head, trying to understand. "Jesus," she said.

"He's had people following me around while I checked things out about your mother." I thought for a moment. "At least he had someone for a while. I think they've quit now."

"You're not the real point," she said. "He still wants to know what I do, even in here. He wants to know who comes to see me. You're the only one." She shivered a little. "He's sick."

"He's just a man who's hung up on you. How does that make him sick?"

"He knows I hate him. I tried to kill him."

"Hate gets close to love. Maybe he doesn't know the difference."

"He told me he'd drop the case against you if I'd hire someone else for my lawyer. He said he'd take care of what's filed against me, that nothing would ever happen, and it would all be forgotten."

"It's up to you," I said, fearing her decision, but unable not to offer the option.

"I guess it's just that I'm not positive any longer," she said reasonably. "He was real good to my mother for a long time. Now, when I think about it, it gets harder and harder to believe he killed her. What good would it do him? There's the money, but he has money. Maybe I was wrong. And now we're both in trouble." She shook her head, trying to clear away the cobwebs of difficulty. "It might be smart to do what he says." She nodded and looked at me, wanting me to decide for her.

I didn't want to decide it for her. It could get easier if I quit—for me—for her. I couldn't help worrying about Monday's hearing. Anything could happen. A loss could hurt. I could be in real trouble. Nevertheless I wasn't going to try ordering her life. She'd have to decide mostly on her own.

I thought about those miles of high fence around the Watts place, the wide road that ran there, the watcher with glasses, the muddy construction. I thought about everything I'd found so far. Something big was going on. The real estate transfers showed that. I just couldn't figure out what it was. Yet.

But Watts wanted me out.

"I don't want anything to happen to you," she said.

I smiled at her. "People have been pushing and pulling at me all of my adult life, Mary Ann. I'm still here. I'll be here after this time is past. If I'm to advise you then I'd say we go ahead through Monday and, when that's over, we'll think about the future. Wait till the hearing's over. If Watts has enough power just to say dismiss and dismiss it is then he can fix things *after* my Monday hearing."

She lowered her eyes and, after a long time, she nodded. "All right," she said. "Am I to be there for your hearing?"

I thought about that. "I don't think so. There's no need. But I'll send word to you when it's done."

She nodded. I'd made the decision and so she dismissed it for now. She got up and moved from the bed to a hard chair, closer to me.

In a very small voice she said: "Someone told me that you were married once, Don."

"Who told you that? Watts?"

"No. Just someone." She looked away from me and I thought she wasn't telling the truth. "I don't remember who it was."

If I'd checked him he'd also probably checked me. By now

he'd know everything he could find out about me. He'd wanted to buy me out on the road—known I was shy of money. He'd use anything he could.

I said: "It was like a bad vaccination. A long time ago now. Is it important?"

She shook her head quickly and smiled at me. I saw that one of her eyeteeth was slightly crooked and I was entranced by it, more than I would have been by perfection.

"I've gone with a lot of men," she admitted, trying to give me something in trade for her knowledge of my lost marriage.

I smiled at her.

Later, at the cell door, when I was leaving we touched hands. No kiss, but the touch was oddly more intimate.

When I left the jail I thought I spied a familiar figure hunched in a parked car near my own.

At the corner lights I was sure. It was Polly. He seemed unsure whether to follow me or stay watching the jail. I saw him look back at the jail building several times.

I went to Bington's one lonely movie house and we watched a science fiction movie I'm sure none of the three of us understood, Polly, me, or the director of the film.

There was this huge, thinking blob in space, see, and he/she/it . . .

I'd gone on impulse, so that when Polly reported back they could sweat about me coolly going to a movie.

Afterward I drove to my apartment and he stayed behind me until I'd gotten settled in for the night. I could see him out the window. He was parked up near the corner under the elm tree that shades the street light.

I wondered why they'd gone back to watching me after getting lax on it.

The Senator died about halfway through my night of dreams. I slept. He died.

He died hard, according to Handy Monday, who was there when I arrived early in the morning. Monday awakened me by phone call just after six.

They'd found him earlier than normally they would have discovered him because a sudden April shower in the very early morning had wet down Bington's streets and blown open the door of his old house. A milkman had spied him collapsed inside on his oaken floor and called the police.

Dr. Hugo Buckner was still there when I arrived. He looked very tired and dispirited.

"He'd been gone a long while by the time I got here, Don," he whispered to me, somehow apologizing for the Senator's death.

"What was it?" I asked numbly.

"If I had to guess I'd guess heart. All the signs are there. Probably a massive attack. I'd guess it took him quickly. The only thing that might warn him would be a little dizziness, some shortness of breath. The pain wouldn't last long, if he felt it at all." He shook his head. "He knew he was on borrowed time. He was in the office a few weeks back. I told him he had maybe a year, maybe even less. I don't think he cared any more. He suffered some fairly constant pain from the chronic angina condition. I gave him some pills for that."

I nodded and moved on. Handy Monday was in the other room and I joined him. He had his little notepad out and was jotting things down in it. His long face was somber.

I said: "Thanks for calling me." Together, we avoided looking at the covered lump on the floor. The Senator was gone. The thing on the floor signified nothing.

"I got here a little while ago," he said. "Milkman called

the station and they sent the emergency squad. Too late. So I called you."

"Doc Buckner thought it was his heart," I said.

"Yeah. There are a couple of things that need clearing up, though." He looked away from me and pursed his lips. "Do you remember the Senator injuring himself in any way recently?"

I shook my head. "I don't know. He could have. He wouldn't have told me. Sometimes he wasn't very steady on his feet."

"The doc found some bruises around his abdominal area."

"How recent?"

"He didn't think they could be more than one day old," he answered carefully.

"Maybe he fell and that helped bring on the attack," I reasoned.

"Sure," he said, and nodded.

"Doc Buckner said that's what he thought it was—a heart attack," I said stubbornly.

He made another cryptic note on his pad, smiled vaguely at me, and turned away.

I walked over and lifted the blanket. His old face was dark and congested. The lips were drawn tightly together as if he were, for the thousandth time, toughing it through. His eyes were wide open. They seemed to want to share with me the wonder of what had happened. All done. All finished.

I let fall the blanket and looked around the room, really looked for the first time.

There were faint red mud stains on the carpet, leading toward the door.

"Damn it to hell," I said so softly that no one could hear, not wanting anyone to hear. I stood there and ached inside, trying to keep that ache locked in. The room was too hot, too close.

Doc Buckner was suddenly there and had me strongly by the arm. He looked at Handy Monday and shook his head.

"I've got a bottle in the car," Doc said. He led me into the cool of the morning and gave me whiskey neat from a bottle. The liquor boiled all the way down.

"Better now?" he asked.

I nodded.

He looked in my eyes and saw I was there again.

"Could it have been something other than a heart attack?" I asked.

"No. And the bruises couldn't have brought it on. If someone gave them to him *that* might have excited him, made him angry, raised his blood pressure, and so precipitated an attack." He looked away from me, up at the clearing sky. "Or he could have fallen." He looked back. "Who should we call to get him? What funeral home?"

I shook my head. "I don't know. His closest surviving relatives left are some cousins. There's one who works at the public library."

"Verna Robbins?"

"Yes."

———◆———

Later, but still very early, I went to the office. I went in, but left the lock on. Virginia had been called, so I knew she wouldn't be in.

I went into his office and sat in the swivel chair. The cushion had begun to break down and was lumpy. I wondered how he'd stood sitting on it.

He had some books out. They were stacked on the desk. I opened several of them and checked the cases he'd indicated with yellow slips. He'd been reading about condemnation rights, who had the right to condemn, what could and could not be subject to condemnation.

I looked out his window and saw his town out there and it didn't mean a thing to me.

It was time to move on. A few months back an old classmate had contacted me. There was an impending opening in his firm. He'd made it plain that when the opening was available I could have first shot. I'd been flattered, but noncommittal.

If the job was still open and I took him up on it I could close things out here in a few months, spread what work there was here and there, then move on. My friend who'd made the offer had mentioned sums of money I wasn't used to, and there could be a new town, new friends, a new car. Maybe Mary Ann would join me, maybe not. I still thought I could deal for a suspended sentence—or someone could.

Bington was done for me. Without the Senator I was a casualty. Joe Watts could and would splinter me up and hang my remains where they could be viewed as an example by the next rebel.

He and his friends owned Bington.

So finish things and move on.

A very few things stood in my way. I did like the town, or at least had liked it. I kept remembering how it appeared from the very top of the hills that bordered it, just before the trip down into the valley where the town crowded. It looked good.

Then there was the Senator.

Someone always wins and someone always loses. The world needs half of each. The results were tallied and I was behind and it seemed easy to give up the game now that my captain was out of it.

I thought about the red stains on the rug. Handy had seen them too, I was sure. I remembered the bruises and the wide, staring eyes.

No decisions for now. Not about leaving, anyway.

Maybe, if they had visited him in his old house, they'd only meant to scare him.

I walked down to the police station. The local radio station must already have had the report of the Senator's death on the early morning news, for people stopped me several times on my way. Some were his friends, but at least half of those who stopped me were only eager for a blow by blow description of his death. Small town collectors and spreaders of bad news.

City Hall seemed semi-deserted, but Handy sat in his office. I sat across the desk from him.

"Coffee?" he asked.

"No thanks," I said. "Not now anyway. Where'd that mud at the Senator's place come from, Handy? There was a similar patch in our office when it was vandalized."

"It's mud that can be found all over this part of the state," he said. "No real way to localize it."

"I know where there's a lot of it available for tracking. They're doing some construction work out there on the land Joe Watts used to own."

"Used to own?" he asked.

"He transferred it to some corporation two days before Mary Ann's mother was killed. She signed the deeds along with Watts. I'm going to get some mileage out of the fact she signed them and then wound up dead. I'm also thinking seriously of hiring some lie detector people to come in here and run tests on Mary Ann, then publicly dare Watts and his crew to also submit to them."

"They don't have to take lie detector tests," he said. "I'm sure they know it."

"That's right," I said. "But I'm going to do it, anyway."

He shook his head thoughtfully. "You don't fight very legally."

"But I'm still going to fight," I said.

"I think you're wrong about Mrs. Watts and about Joe Watts. I've known him for a long time, back all the way to the Detroit days. He's a ruthless man, but I can't believe he'd be a party to hurting or killing someone."

I leaned back in my spindly chair. Maybe its insecurity was meant to trouble a suspect. It groaned under my weight.

"Did you check out that license number?"

He nodded. "Watts's similar number in the next state south. State chairman. I called down there to check out why he was visiting the Watts place and was told he was on party business. Within half an hour of my call both the mayor and the prosecutor were in here telling me to keep my nose in my own business."

"How well did you know Watts in Detroit?"

"I knew him a little. Before I went on the police force up there I worked at one of the auto plants. Watts was head man in the test department. He was miles beyond me, a big stockholder, a man to watch, but I knew him. I quit before he had his rounds with the company." He shook his head. "In a way you might say he brought me down here to Bington." He looked away. "After things went bad up there."

"Why? Did he call you to come down here?"

He laughed. "No. It wasn't like that." He looked at me

and I thought he'd said more than he wanted already, but now he felt he had to explain. "I knew he was down here is all. I just more or less wandered in. Him being here meant nothing. I called him. He helped me get on the police force here. Not that it required a lot of pull. They were short-handed."

"Is he a friend?"

"No. I'm a realist. I try to get along with him."

"What would you do if I was able to show you he'd done something wrong, Handy?"

Something changed in his eyes. "Show me that and he's the same as everyone else—at least to me."

I sat there watching him and I had a sudden hunch that he wasn't telling me anything near all of it.

"You say you don't believe he'd hurt anyone?" I asked carefully.

He nodded slowly, not looking at me.

"I don't believe that, Handy. I think the reason, or at least one reason, why you wound up here in Bington is that you thought he might have had something to do with the death of your wife and son."

He was up and around the desk. He caught my right shoulder in a clutching grip, mangling it.

"Don't say anything like that, you bastard. Don't ever say it."

His eyes were almost closed and he was breathing hard. I stood quietly until he unloosed me.

"I don't ever think about that any more," he said to both of us.

"You're going to have to talk to me," I said.

He shook his head adamantly. "Not with anyone."

"I need to know, Handy. I deserve to know."

He went back to his chair and sat in it. For a while I didn't think he was going to say anything.

He said: "I thought maybe he was the one."

I leaned forward, straining to hear his voice.

"I was working a special detail up there when it happened. It was a conspiracy to take over the plant where Watts worked. He was part of it. It would have been nothing to us if he did it through the stock market, but there was some other stuff. Two men got killed in an accident at his plant. I never could tie him to it, but I thought he was part of that, too."

"Were you involved in the investigation?"

"Yes. The word got out on the rigging thing. I suppose I helped it get out. Things got complicated on the stock and Watts and his group didn't get the price they wanted and when they tried to buy back in the price had gone up rather than down. He gave it up and came down here." He gave me a quick look. "It was far more complicated than that, but that was the core of it. The companies up there spy on each other and even on themselves. It's a fast world."

He fell silent so I prompted him: "And your wife and son?"

"He was out of the country by the time the car was bombed." He looked at me and there was nothing at all in his eyes. "But it got to be a dead end up there. Once, in the investigation, I heard his name. So when I left I came down here. It was a dead end here, too. But there was some peace here. Even after I was fairly well satisfied, I stayed."

I said: "I think it's peculiar. You do Watts a disfavor and you wind up losing by it. I do something he doesn't want me to do and I wind up losing. Maybe it's just a bad thing to be on his hate list. Maybe he's got some people who watch over him."

He shook his head. "There's no evidence." He tapped his hand on the desk for emphasis. "I had a crew all over the Senator's part of town this morning asking questions. No one saw anything. No one heard anything. The Senator was an old man. Maybe he drug the mud in himself. Maybe he fell or something, like you said. There isn't a thing to show that it was anything other than natural death."

"All right," I said.

"Find me something," he said. "I got time to wait."

"Maybe I can," I said. "It makes you wonder, don't it?"

"What?"

"How a man like Watts can get to the top?"

"He's smart, Don. But that isn't really my problem or yours."

"Yes it is," I said. "It sure is."

He eyed me without comprehension for a second and then he grudgingly nodded.

I got up to leave, but he stopped me with a wave of his hand. He dug back in his drawer and came up with a big blue steel revolver. He snapped the cylinder out and inspected the loads.

"Here," he said. "Take this."

"No," I said, but I was tempted for a moment. "Not me, Handy. If I had it I might use it and I don't ever want to have to do it that way again."

"That's right. You were in the war. You just remember I offered."

The Union Hall was open, but Ward Younger wasn't around. I took a seat inside on a folding chair and stared around the barren room.

I heard him pull up outside. He has an old clanker that

makes my Plymouth look good. I opened his hall door, surprising him, and bowed him in.

He grinned sourly at me.

There isn't a lot of union activity in Bington. Somehow local industry has managed to stave the unions off, slander them to the workers, openly fight them when they begin to gain strength, and shut down the plants when the unions win a voice. Bington remains a bastion against union activity, but the unions still try from time to time to break in. What little activity there is centers around Ward Younger.

He's a nice guy and we're friends. Once, not too long ago, I did him a turn when he was flat and down and he's never forgotten it. A family thing. He and his wife are still together and it looks like a lifetime contract again now.

He led me to his office. It occupied a tiny corner of the drafty Union Hall. There was an old desk, three chairs, and a couple of filing cabinets.

He sat down at his desk, grinning at me now, and opened a drawer. He withdrew an ancient green eyeshade and perched it on top of his balding head.

"You look like the last of the red hot crap shooters," I said.

"I couldn't make even one pass if my life depended on it," he said. He tapped his eyeshade. "Keeps the glare down from all these bright lights." He looked up at the one lonely light fixture. "Part of my clown act. Us union executives all have one to put people at ease."

I laughed politely.

"There's got to be something you need," he said. "What can I do for you?"

"I want to know what's under construction out on Joe Watts's place up near the north end of the county?"

He got out a pipe and put it in his mouth, cold.

"If you can tell me without compromising anything," I added, while he was thinking.

"Okay. He came in here and hired some people. I thought maybe he was going to build a dam for a lake." He shook his head, trying to clear his memory. "No one told me what it was when they were hired. They just come in for ten men at first. Later, it was twenty. They've got some bulldozers, too."

"Maybe a subdivision?"

"I swear I ain't ever heard, Don. Give me a little time and I'll try to check it for you."

"I haven't got much time," I said.

"Quick as I can, then."

"How long's he had men working out there?"

"Wait a minute and I'll find out." He got up, still sucking his cold pipe. He took a manila folder from one of the filing cabinets and looked inside it."

"Eight weeks tomorrow." He closed the folder and put it back. "I did hear one thing, which ain't my business, but which I'll pass on. They got dogs out there and a guy sits up on the roof with a gun."

"Check for me and see if you can find out from any of your folks what he's supposed to be doing and then call me," I said.

"Sure," he said. "I'll find out for you."

Assuming the necessity, the way to get over a ten-foot fence is with a taller ladder. At a discount store, top of the hill, braving hordes of women in for the gigantic spring sale, I bought a twelve-foot aluminum ladder. I stripped it of tags and tied it to the side of my Plymouth. If they were following me I saw no sign of them. I parked the car behind the building, out of sight. I took the ladder in with me.

The afternoon Bington *Chronicle* had headlines about the death of the Senator. There was a long article that detailed his life and the political offices he'd held. His ancestors had been among Bington's early settlers. The paper got into that and, in an editorial, said he was a good friend, that the loss was tragic, and that the town would miss him.

He'd despised the paper.

I read everything carefully. There wasn't a hint there was anything amiss in his death.

His funeral was set for Monday afternoon, the afternoon of my trial in city court. By that time I could be in bad problems. His service was to be in the pleasant Presbyterian church his great-great-grandfather had helped construct a century and a half back.

I turned on my little apartment television when I grew restless. The Reds dropped a close one to the Braves. I wasn't that much interested, but it was something to do to use up the Saturday afternoon.

When the ballgame was finished I sat there still looking at the television, but not really seeing it. I remembered the dog I'd seen behind the fence. It had looked both savage and efficient. Ward Younger had said there were dogs, plural. I wondered how many there were. I'd have to stay away from them, not let them smell me or see me.

There was also the problem of the electric fence, but maybe the ladder could take care of that.

Once the Senator had been a compulsive walker, one of those people who walk miles daily for exercise and the love of walking. He'd infected me. When he'd had to stop he'd given me his special walking cane for dogs. I'd never used it, for dogs will not normally bother me. But guard dogs were something different.

I went to my closet and opened it and rummaged until I found the cane. The batteries were dead, but I could buy fresh ones. I doubted the cane would repulse a determined dog. It was, however, better than being empty-handed.

In the closet I also found my old service binoculars and took them out too.

The phone rang several times, but I wouldn't answer it. I spent the free time working theories through my head about what lay behind that fence. Assuming that Mary Ann's mother had been killed by Joe Watts, could it have been because of what was hidden in/on those two thousand acres?

When the sun began to fade I drove to a drugstore up on the hill. I watched behind me, but saw no one. The ladder clanked against the side of the car. I got fresh batteries and loaded my metal-tipped cane. I took the Plymouth up the interstate and turned off a mile below the exit to Watts's place. Half a mile north I found a gravel road that led back to the commune near Joe Watts's land. The spring rains had washed the gravel into the ditches and the road needed dragging, but it was passable. All the way I kept watch behind me, but if there was a follower I saw nothing.

I almost missed the commune entrance because the weeds had taken over, but I spotted it at the last instant and steered the Plymouth into the opening.

They lived in a slatternly old house. This year I counted nine in residence. At least there were nine out back of the house digging in the soft, familiarly red earth. I saw four boys, four girls, and one I wasn't gender sure of in my counting. In the years I'd known about the commune the population had been as high as twenty and as low as five.

They live together and maybe it means something to them, gives them security or love. To me it seems a step back rather than a step up, but I've learned tolerance.

Several of the diggers knew me well enough to calm the others.

The one I knew best was a boy called "Hoff." His real name was unrelated to the nickname, something long and foreign. He nodded at me and stopped his spade.

"Hello, Mr. Robak," he said.

He was emaciated and I could almost see the back of his skull through his translucent eyes. One of the others once told me Hoff had spent a long, agonizing time in a prison camp in Vietnam. I don't know whether it was one of ours or one of theirs. Hoff had long hair and a sparse beard and there was a tic at the far edge of his right eye. He was scrupulously clean, not easy in a house that I knew was without running water. I liked him.

I held out my hand and he took it tentatively, knowing I sought something. I could almost see him going over what I'd done for him and the commune as he stood there, watching me.

The others went back to digging, content to leave me to Hoff.

"Is it all right if I park my car behind the house where it can't be seen from the road and walk over your farm to the next road north?"

He considered. "Is there trouble in it?"

"Perhaps," I said. "I'd doubt that any of the trouble could come to you people."

He considered some more and then nodded. "You've been our friend more than once. We won't stop you, but we won't help you if trouble comes." He put out his thin, but strong hand and touched my shoulder. He looked in my eyes and saw something there. "If it's gone bad then we invite you to stay here with us for a time. When there are others around to share troubles then those troubles become easier to live with. The turmoil recedes."

I experienced unanticipated temptation. I had the urge to quit making decisions, to hide from problems. But there was Mary Ann to think of and the Senator to remember. The moment passed.

He saw its passage in my eyes. Both of us knew I was too old and too square. I was born to be a Rotarian, a member of the Chamber of Commerce.

And so he nodded and smiled vaguely at me and turned away to the land again.

I made sure the car couldn't be seen from the road while they ignored me. I untied the ladder and walked toward the tree line. When I reached it I turned back for a moment. Hoff rose up from his digging, saw me, gave the ladder a covetous look, and waved without meaning. I waved back.

The ladder was light, but clumsy. I discovered that as the undergrowth became thicker I had to plan ahead on how the ladder would be handled. Sometimes I had to raise it high, sometimes I had to carry it low or slide it between branched areas.

It took a good half an hour to move up to the far edge of the commune land. When I got close to the crest of the hill that overlooked Joe Watts's house I let the ladder drop. I'd tied the cane to it. It wasn't time to use either of them yet and I didn't want to carry them with me to the top of the hill. Someone might see the sun reflecting from the ladder or cane tip and so spot me.

I proceeded carefully up the hill, keeping to cover. At the

brow of the hill, after some searching, I found a likely spot to set up watch. From it I could see the front of the house clearly. I could also see some of the area that was under construction.

I settled in. My vantage place was near an old, densely branched tree. The ground was cold and there was a brisk wind. The sun was pleasant however and I estimated the temperature to be in the high 50s. Hardy flying insects occasionally buzzed through the air. Some of them discovered me and explored both me and the area I'd taken over, but I wasn't excessively bothered.

With a pencil I dug an exploratory hole in the earth at my side. The soil was red. Across the asphalt road, in the construction area, the bare earth was the same color of red. Senator's carpet red. Office window-sill red.

I took the binoculars and examined the house. It was three stories, expensively constructed of brick and stone. There was a long, paved asphalt drive that led from the huge gate to a circular area that fronted the house. Everything was lavishly landscaped. Near the house there were gardens filled with early flowers. I trained the glasses on the garden areas. The flowers, seen from the better view, were growing wild, untended.

The windows of the house were curtained and all the curtains were drawn.

A man sat on the third-floor porch.

I again recognized Alvin Suedell. He wore heavy shoes, checked slacks, and a windbreaker. He had his own set of binoculars. A rifle was leaned negligently against the porch rail. The construction area was Saturday afternoon empty today and so he wasn't watching it. He used the binoculars instead to inspect the road outside the fence and keep watch on all of Watts's land. Once, when a solitary car passed on the blacktop below me, he watched it carefully until it was completely out of sight.

He seldom relaxed. He kept the binoculars moving. Now and then he'd kick a leg up over the porch rail to steady his stance. When he did that I could see red mud clinging to the bottom of his shoe. The first time I saw it a wave of anger washed over me and burned my insides, but I just felt cold from then on. I stayed low to the ground and watched the watcher.

From my angle I could see a part of the swimming pool. It was full of water. A side wall had been cranked a foot or so open to admit some of the brisk April air. A plastic dome covered the pool area and slid with the wall.

The construction area was a very fuzzy thing to me. Bulldozers had laid out wide trails. Those trails might be for streets and the stakes along the trails might indicate lot lines. The bulldozers were pulled off by the trees today. I studied the construction area, or what I could see of it, for a long time. No idea came to me other than the idea that it might be subdivision type construction.

The garage attached to the house was fully occupied, indicating that Joe Watts was in residence. The garage contained a familiar-looking low-slung foreign car, a utilitarian jeep with muddy tires, a new, shiny Corvette, plus the Rolls. The Rolls was parked in the far corner of the garage. I could still see the scars it bore from my encounter with it. I'd crumpled in one side badly.

As I watched Joe Watts entered the garage from some unseen door. Polly accompanied him. They walked to where the Rolls was parked. I noted, with slightly mixed feelings, that Polly was still limping a little. Seeing Polly reminded me of one of the Senator's sayings: *That'll teach them to mess around with the Lone Ranger.* Thinking of his tired, old saying made me sad all over again. I wondered if I'd perhaps never seen Mary Ann, or, seeing her, had refused her case, if the Senator would be alive now. I admitted it was a good possibility.

I was adult enough to know that life can't be lived that way, child enough to wish it could.

Down below Watts gesticulated to Polly about the car. I could see Watts's hands clench and unclench with anger as he inspected my damage. I doubted it was the first time he'd inspected the car.

Under direction from Watts, Polly finally got into the Rolls and backed it out of the garage and drove down the drive. He unlocked the gate and drove through it, then got out and relocked. He drove on. I watched for a long time. Far away I could see the rise of the interstate road. Watts's road made a bend and a dip there and I lost the Rolls. I never did see it enter the four-lane and I finally quit looking for it, not sure where Polly had gone, but suspicious about what had happened, maybe even a little alarmed.

Joe Watts walked around outside his big house for a little while and then went back in. He seemed restless to me. Several times he scanned the road in front of me and the hill where I lay hidden, but I was certain he couldn't see me. He was either a man who was very aware and suspicious or a man with very acute senses, able to sense the hunter. It could be only that he believed that someone, and perhaps me, would be calling upon him, would be watching, and so he was waiting, set and ready. Or maybe they'd gone looking for me and not found me.

They might even already know where I was.

I drew back a little. It was now beginning to get along toward dusk.

I watched the house very carefully and was rewarded when, in the dim light, I caught a hint of movement at the front window. Watts had opened the curtain there a fraction and I could see him crouched a little, scanning the road again. I knew he couldn't see me, but his very intentness was scary, as if he knew I was out there. I hunched low, completely out of sight for a long time.

When I took courage and risked another look the curtains were drawn tight again. I resumed my inspection.

I found a possibility down the road, perhaps a quarter mile away. There was an old tree that grew inside the fence. The fence line had been cleared almost up to the tree. A huge, gnarled branch extended out over the fence.

As I watched a dog passed the tree, very silent, slipping from shadow to shadow. I wasn't sure it was the same dog I'd seen before, but there was bound to be more than one dog.

The wind blew gently toward me, but once I got over that fence and toward the house that same wind would carry my scent back to a dog trailing along the fence.

I had a very bad feeling inside me. I tried to come up with just what I was doing here. Watts, behind his fence, was waiting for me, expecting me probably. The whole picture indicated he was preparing for a visit and ready for it. I figured that the reason I hadn't seen the Rolls again was because it was in wait for me at a pull-off spot down the road.

The Senator had told me several times that I wasn't some tough detective. I could almost hear him whispering his advice in my ear again. Even if I got over the fence and remained undiscovered and found something then that something would be of little value to me or to Mary Ann. If I obtained evidence by my own illegal act then such evidence would not be admissible. I had no legal right beyond that fence.

I sat there and tried to think like the Senator and, after a while, I became a sane, rational man again. They knew I was coming and I didn't want to waste that entirely.

I took the field glasses and, in the last of the light, studied the construction area and the house once more. Nothing new was happening at the house, no open drapes, no action. Sue had vanished from the top of the porch.

The construction had to be the layout for a gigantic subdivision. It looked more like that than anything I could cudgel up.

The thing to do was to make them think I'd been inside their damned fence, make them insecure.

The wind grew cold and the insects hid for the night. Lights came on all around the big house. The side of the pool which had been open closed on silent, oiled tracks and soft lights played on the mirror of water.

Powerful lights also came on behind the fence, illuminating the areas that bordered it. The spot around the tree I'd targeted was shadowed somewhat by the trunk and branches.

I moved out. I left the ladder, but I untied the cane and took it. I stayed down below the edge of the hill and in deep shadow until I got close to the area of the fence I wanted.

I took out my handkerchief and wiped all of the surfaces of the cane, not even forgetting the batteries. I flipped the switch to "on." Keeping in the shadow of the tree trunk as much as I could I approached the fence and hurled the cane up over the fence, hoping that the force of landing would not switch off the power. Somewhere, far away, I heard a dog whine. When I was up the side of the second hill, hurrying back toward the commune with the ladder, I heard a dog's yelp of pain. I increased my speed.

I left the ladder in plain sight for the commune kids. They could use it. It had been hard to transport it back through the darkness, but I felt a sense of accomplishment at bringing it back for them. Lights were on in the house and someone was strumming a stringed instrument and others were singing. I stopped for a moment and listened. It was an old song about unrequited love and sudden death.

I went to the Plymouth and started up and drove back to Bington without incident.

After dressing in my best suit I went to the funeral home. I'm not really much of a funeral-home buff, but I went there.

The Senator's distant relatives sat in chairs near the raised bier where his body was on view. Virginia huddled in the midst of the relatives. The relatives chattered among themselves like birds at a morning fountain.

Everything seemed to slow down when I came in.

Verna Robbins was the only relative I knew even casually. She was a tiny woman with a long thin nose and aristocratic eyes. She'd never approved of me. Once I'd represented her ex-husband after he'd been convicted of murder and I'd eventually gotten him off. I'd heard she'd expressed doubts about both of us after that.

She arose and came up to me, her fine eyes wary. I think she was remembering that I sometimes bit.

"My sympathies," I said, in the accepted formula.

She relaxed and nodded at me. She took my hand tightly and led me up to the coffin so I could see.

"He looks very good, doesn't he?" she asked.

He didn't look good. He was dead. But I nodded.

"How's Virginia doing?" I asked.

"She'll be all right. She comes of good stock, that woman. I'm going to stay the night with her." She frowned and shook her head. "I wouldn't say anything to her tonight," she confided. "She's still quite upset."

Virginia was blaming me of course. Maybe she was right.

"The funeral's Monday afternoon?"

"Yes. At half after two. And you're to be one of the pallbearers," she said.

"He left a note of instructions," she added firmly.

I nodded. I'd have bet he probably grinned when he wrote out that note knowing that it would make me miserable and that I must do it all at the same time.

People were coming in. The room was getting crowded. Verna Robbins left me to greet others. I stood where I was for a time, looking now and then at Virginia, but she wouldn't look back at me.

I eased to the back of the room. At the entry door I met Governor Bratewell coming in. He was accompanied by a state trooper.

"Hey," he said amiably to me. "We're sure missing you up there."

"Thanks," I said. He meant in the jolly state legislature. But no one really misses you there once you leave. They take up clubs and harsh words against your successor instead of you.

He leaned toward me. "I'm sorry about the Senator. He was an old friend and I'll miss him a lot." He ignored the people doing double takes as they gawked past him. "He called not too long ago and I talked to him. I'm glad of that."

The state policeman tugged politely, but firmly at his elbow and pointed at his watch. Governor Bratewell nodded at me and moved on. I followed along and waited until I could get his eye again.

"You said the Senator called," I whispered to him. "Can you remember what exactly he wanted?"

He frowned, trying to remember. There'd been a thousand phone calls and he'd been picked at and pursued since the Senator's call, but he was equal to the task of remembering. He nodded. "He wanted to know about Joe Watts. He asked me a lot of questions about Joe." He grinned and lost ten years from his apparent age. "Joe's a man with big ideas."

"That's right," I agreed. "But what was it he wanted to know about Joe Watts?"

"He wanted to know if anything could be on the drawing board for this part of the state. I told him that I didn't know of anything at all. I also told him that other people sometimes knew about things like that long before I did." He turned away and then back. "I did tell him I'd heard they were secretly hunting around for an area jetport to take care of big jet traffic, assuming we can get gas enough for them. That isn't coming through this state and the site hasn't been chosen yet. I understand there are a lot of areas being considered." The state policeman tugged again, reminding him of the schedule. He nodded at me once more and turned away.

As I went out the door Lou Calberg was entering. He gave my suit an expert's look.

"That suit fits you good, Don. You must have bought it at my place."

I smiled. "Come with me for a moment."

"All right. I'm sorry about the Senator."

I led him outside and to the Plymouth. I dug under the

seat where I'd left them and gave him the copy of the agreement between Watts and his deceased wife.

"Hide that someplace."

He raised his eyebrows a little, but he took the document and put it in his pocket and nodded at me.

"Thanks, Lou," I said.

"For nothing," he said, and smiled. He patted my shoulder and went back across the street to the funeral home.

I stood watching him. An old car pulled up behind me as I watched and a horn beeped discreetly at me. It was Ward Younger, my union friend.

He had his window cranked down and he grinned out at me.

"Way I get it from the boys is that Watts is supposed to be subdividing about fifteen hundred acres into estate-size building lots. My boys have been bulldozing out the proposed roads and laying out the flags where the lot lines are supposed to be."

I whistled softly. "Fifteen hundred acres will make a lot of estates."

"Everybody wants their own empire. The way Ed Day, and he's the one who told me about it, had it explained is that there will be police at the gate and no one gets in without living there or being invited there. Going to run their own commuter buses for the inhabitants. And no seekers of charity permitted, no salesmen. I hear that sort of thing isn't too unusual these days."

I nodded slowly. He'd be selling the land in the big cities. The nearest big city was forty miles, but the roads to it were superb. Commuter buses, cocktail transportation, the good life. Far from the madding crowd.

"One more thing," Younger said, snapping his fingers. "Ed

said that at first he was paid by Watts himself. But some weeks back the name on the check changed and he was paid by a corporation check on an outfit called the Bington Home Developers. I ain't never heard of them, for whatever that means. But the checks have been good."

"Thanks," I said.

"Is the corporation just Watts under a beard?"

"I don't know—yet." I looked him over. "Thanks, Ward. Thanks a lot."

He grinned and drove off leaving me in a cloud of exhaust. I went over to the Plymouth and got in it and drove down by the river and parked. It was too early for pleasure craft and this year of shortages might turn out lean, but upriver I could see a towboat coming down, the pilot sweeping the shore with a powerful beam of light as he sought deep water. The river was still up and there was drift along the shores, but summer was coming. Then people would come to sample for a day or two what I had all year. The college kids would flee Bington, unaware of what they missed. Lou Calberg proudly told me one day that when the Lord made the Garden of Eden he designed Bington the same day for Eden's vacation spot.

Sitting there in my afflicted old car it seemed hard to see all the way ahead to summer without the Senator.

I tried not to let his loss affect my feelings about Mary Ann. The thing to do was to be angry at those who'd caused his death and to be bright enough to throw a lot of pepper in the soup they had cooking.

The Senator was an old man with a bad heart.

But surely they'd come into his house and frightened him until he died, bullied him to death.

I slept pretty well considering. In dreams the Senator came and tried to tell me exactly what had happened, but he could only speak a language I couldn't understand. When I reached to touch him he'd turn shadowy. I kept coming awake and then slipping back down into uneasy sleep.

I got out early on Sunday morning and went in search of a Sunday paper, yawning all the way.

I found a paper at an early opening grocery and came back, fixed coffee, and drank it black while I read the paper. I read about the supreme court's latest chewable verdict, full of high purpose. I read and smiled. Someplace Holmes and Cardozo and Marshall must be shaking their heads and laughing. But it's the court's world and the rest of us must learn to live in it. Or try.

I turned on television and watched a girl trying to sell her brand of diet cola. It was apparent from looking her over that her only real need in reducing might be an inch or two off her brassiere size.

They are laughable on television ads these days. Honest finance companies offer to lend you that money just because they love you, cars are hundreds of dollars cheaper from dealer-advertiser, and aspirin and buffered aspirin will cure everything from headaches to hangnails. One can't have a decent sex life without the right soap, shaver, deodorant, and gentle ladies must smuggle their own toilet paper into visited homes.

I finished my coffee and the most of the paper and called Handy Monday. He answered on ring two.

"You got any time to talk to me today?"

"Sure. Fishing or drinking?"

"If anything, drinking. I don't want to get into much difficulty today. No hangovers. I've a long day coming for me tomorrow."

"Oh," he said, surprise evident in his voice. "Are you going to go ahead with the trial? I thought that with the Senator being gone . . ."

"I'm going ahead."

"You want to come over and talk now?"

I said I did and he told me to come on, so I drove on over.

Handy lives in an apartment complex which rents out one, two or three bedrooms, provides a parking spot for your motor vehicle, and has a swimming pool. It's Bington's finest and caters to everyone, except that its managers have difficulty finding an opening if you're black, yellow, red, an off shade of white, go to church on Brand "X" day, or are just otherwise undesirable.

Handy lives in a splendid apartment that's as bare and sterile as he can unconsciously make it. I've been in the apartment a number of times. The homiest thing about it is the bottle of whiskey Handy keeps in one of the cabinets. I think he refuses to make anything outside his job a part of himself. His home is the police station. He sleeps and bathes at the apartment, and occasionally I think he'll take a casual girl there, make love to her on antiseptic sheets, then make certain that all traces of her once presence are quickly erased.

He had coffee waiting. He handed me a cup.

"Want to go down to the pool for a swim? I've got an extra pair of trunks. Usually there's girls down around there." He gave me a sly smile. "Roba Dickens lives here now, two apartment buildings over. She hangs out around the pool a lot. She asks about you now and then."

I know Roba Dickens. She collects men and hangs them

to dry in her voluminous picture albums. She is camera equipped. To be on a date with her is constantly being asked to pose. She also has an amazing young-old body and a capacity for scotch whiskey I've never seen equaled, plus the finesse of a steam locomotive. A long weekend with Roba and one cold beer would be enough to kill a good, young man. I was glad I was old, glad I'd met her in a previous year, glad that time was past.

I said carefully: "Let's stay here. I wanted to check with you on a few things. And I'd like for you to be around and available in city court in the morning to testify for me if need be."

"You think you'll need me?" he asked.

"I don't know. The special judge either believes me or them. I might need someone around to swear that I'm a halfway honest man."

He nodded. "I'll be around. If I'm not on station then the boys will know where to raise me by radio or telephone."

"Thanks. Now tell me some more about the accident that Joe Watts had in which Alma Watts was killed."

"What do you want to know? I'll assume you've seen the report?"

"I've seen it. How come you checked it instead of, say, someone else?"

He gave me a sour look. "Let's say that I like to keep my eyes on things out that way. The reason should be apparent to you. When the call came through I made the run. In fact when the call came I was north of the Watts place. I came down the interstate and down his big road he talked the county into building. I was the first officer there. So I made out the report."

"The daughter keeps claiming that Watts killed her

mother. I didn't think much of it at first, but so many things have happened that I now think it could have been that way. I know, for example, that I didn't attack Watts. I figure if he'll lie about me because I'm checking him out then he's got something to hide and wants me scared off."

"About that I know nothing," he said. "I suspect, but I know nothing. As to the accident there was nothing that made me walk slow there. He came out the gate and skidded into the tree trunk and she was pure unlucky. Maybe he could have wrecked the car purposely with the idea he'd live through it and she wouldn't, but that would be a chancy thing." He looked up at me. "You know him. Can you believe he'd take that chance?" He thought about it some more and shook his head with finality. "No. Not feasible. He could buy someone to bonk her on the head if he'd wanted her dead. Someone from the old stomping ground."

"The problem there being that if he did just that you might, by chance, recognize the person or persons he imported."

"There would be that," he admitted. "And I think he knows I watch him some still."

"What do you know about Alma Watts before or after her marriage that might interest me?"

"Nothing I guess. She dated here and there. She was a damned good-looking woman." He grinned suddenly at me. "I asked her out on a date once. She told me she was too old for me. She was gentle and nice about it, but it hurt my ego. And you know our prosecutor had a real thing going with her for a short time until he chickened out. And don't let him kid you that he didn't know who she was. He knew all right. He'd have to know." He gave me a look. "She was a bunch of woman. Think how Mary Ann will look in ten or fifteen years if everything goes right for her, then add a little, and you'll get an idea of how she looked." His voice lowered. "The wreck busted her all up. She must have gone straight into the door post. It put a groove in her skull like an alley between buildings. She was dead when I got there. Probably instantaneous. Shame."

"How was he?"

"Unconscious, but not bad hurt. They ambulanced him into the clinic, cleaned him up a little, gave him a sedative when he turned a little hysterical, and sent him home. No hits, no runs, no errors. He was alive and she was dead."

"They signed a bunch of deeds like two days before and he was going to have to give her a big chunk of money if they got divorced according to their marriage agreement." I looked at him. "Convenient, wasn't it?"

"How much money?"

"Six hundred thousand dollars. Maybe he learned to trick drive a car up in Detroit, drive it good enough to kill her?"

He shook his head. "He was an executive, not some kind of stunt driver. You don't like him. I don't like him either. I've been keeping watch on him for a long time. You believe he had your office busted up, that he filed a false and spiteful affidavit against you and maybe killed the Senator. Makes it hard for both of us to be logical, but I'm going to try for both of us. Because both of us know that you don't have a bit of hard evidence against him." He held up a hand silencing my reply. "You've caused the man problems. He fights anyone who gets in his way and you're in it. But you're going to have to show me something to get me to go much further."

"All right," I said. "I'll accept that for the moment because it isn't something I can really argue with successfully.

I'm trying to pin down some of that hard evidence. That's why I'm asking you about the wreck."

"Ask away."

"How soon after the wreck happened were you there?"

He shrugged. "I don't remember for sure. A bit of time, ten, maybe fifteen minutes."

"Was Watts still in the car?"

"No. They'd taken him out."

"Who took him out?"

"One of the people who works for him. No one saw the accident, but they heard it. Ted Polly was there before me. So was Alvin Suedell. One of them took him out." He waved a hand. "As far as time's concerned, if there's fraud involved, if I was lied to, the accident could have taken place a considerable while before it was reported. I questioned Polly and Suedell and Watts. They set the time." He gave me an irritated look. "What makes you think it wasn't an accident? Riddle me that."

"Not one solid thing. All I've really got to go on is a nightmare witnessed by a girl who's either a murderer or insane. Plus all the vicious and screwball things that have happened since." I clenched my hands. "Even if Watts did kill her and Mary Ann didn't kill one Roger Tuttle why would Watts continue to raise a stench with me and mine? It's purely stupid for him to do it because I won't quit. I can't quit."

"Do you have anything to show that Mary Ann didn't kill Roger Tuttle?"

"No," I said. "But I know some things to do which are going to be quite unpleasant. After she's been examined by my psychiatrist—one I hire—then I'm thinking about some lie detector evidence. If she passes I'm going to scream that her accusers be tested also. And if I lose my trial tomorrow I'm going to go take one and scream again."

He gave me a sober look. "You always have had the ability to make things happen, Don."

I thought dismally about the Senator and gave him no answer.

"Have a drink?" he invited after a while.

"I thought you'd never ask," I joked drearily.

He went to his cupboard and got out his lonely bottle of bourbon, a little dusty, but half full. He sprang ice cubes and dropped them into glasses, working efficiently. I noticed that he made his drink only half as potent as mine. I've never seen him drunk. He guards himself against that sort of thing.

I looked out the apartment windows. From my vantage point I could see the glassed-in building that housed the pool. Although its windows were steamy I imagined I could see Roba inside, oversized at the top, bright hair a tossing challenge to the male world she wanted conquered.

"Drink up," he said, maybe reading my mind. "That'll give you guts enough to borrow one of my swim suits and go with me down to the pool."

I watched him and he grew restless under my glance, maybe knowing that I wanted more from inside him.

"Tell me about what happened in Detroit."

He shook his head firmly. "No. That time is over now. If I bring it to mind, tell you about it, then I'll dream about it for days."

"I lost the Senator, Handy."

"He's gone. They're all gone, Don." He looked away from me and he was silent for a time, but finally he nodded to himself, accepting it.

"Someone put a bomb in the car. It was a pro deal. Nine

sticks, all wired to go off if the starter was pressed or the hood tampered with. She wanted to go to the grocery and she took the car while I was sleeping. I remember her coming in and kissing me, taking the keys out of my pocket. I'd been in and the car had been in the garage for maybe four hours. She took the boy along. When I heard the explosion I thought the world had ended." He looked over at me and gave me a crooked, little smile. "Maybe it did. I went running out. It had blown the boy out of the car. He wasn't dead. It took three days for him to die. The worst thing was that I couldn't get her out of the car. He was out, but she wasn't. I knew he was going to die and the car was on fire . . ."

He stopped, face dreadful.

"You never found out who did it?"

He shook his head. "No. Not really anything. We checked out every person who'd ever been close to anything as big as a firecracker in that town and there was nothing. I heard a lot of names from stoolies, informers. Watts was one of the names. The hit man was someone from out of town. I know that now. Had to be. He probably drove in and drove out. We checked the airlines, trains, and buses for a long time after it happened and never got anything."

"Why did they want to kill you?"

"It's a tough town. I made enemies. Watts wasn't one of the ones who made top of my enemy list. I didn't even consider him for a long time."

"Why did you begin to consider him?"

"His name came up. Plus he moved on, left Detroit. There wasn't anyone else."

"When Watts left the country where did he go?"

He shook his head. "I checked that out. He went to the usual places—London, Paris, Rome. Nothing."

"What do you know about Roger Tuttle, Handy?"

"Not much. He was a flopper. Here and there. A drunk and small-time politician. He could dig out a hundred floaters for them on Election Day. And sometimes you need those hundred votes. Watts gave him a job of sorts. He was a gardener-utility type. Anyway he was sleeping out there at Watts's place. No real loss, but still a human being."

I said: "The thing that bugs me is that the papers and the people pushing this thing seem a lot more shook up that my client took a shot at Boss Watts than that she killed Roger Tuttle."

"Watts is a big man," he said, shrugging.

When I left Handy's apartment I drove to the office. I went again into the Senator's office and sat in his chair. I looked over what was on his desk carefully this time. There were six books out, all page-marked where he'd been reading. For the second time I read the condemnation cases in the marked pages. They had to do with what could and could not be claimed as damages where land was taken under condemnation. Nothing germinated, although I felt something stir at the vague edge of my brain.

The Senator's scratch pad was not very illuminating either. There was a number scribbled on the pad which I recognized as the governor's number.

The only other thing on the scratch pad was a note the Senator had made for himself about my trial tomorrow.

"And then you say I attacked Mr. Watts?" I asked the precisely dressed gentleman who'd been interrogated under the name of Alvin Suedell by a fawning prosecutor. County chairman Suedell.

He'd just cut my wrists on direct. He'd done it well. I almost believed him even though I knew I hadn't been anywhere near the Watts place.

Suedell looked me over. He then inspected the special court stenographer I'd demanded and grudgingly gotten. I could see he didn't trust her rapid pencil and the squiggles she was making on her pad. He was against anything done out of the back room or card room. He looked uncomfortable in the daylight of the city courtroom.

He said carefully: "That's right. Then you hit Mr. Watts. Polly wanted to step in and do something drastic, but Mr. Watts wouldn't let us." He smiled at me and looked past me at Polly. Polly had limped into the courtroom.

I could have asked for a separation of witnesses, but I hadn't done it. I figured they'd already had dress rehearsal on their stories. They wouldn't be bothered or caught by rehearing each other.

The Bington city courtroom held half a crowd. There were the usual number of Monday morning hangers-on, come for the excitement of seeing reckoning taken against the weekend wrongdoers. Today there were representatives of the local press and radio hunting for juicy headlines, here for my unveiling. I figured the prosecution might have invited them.

There was one other viewer. He sat in the back of the room. I knew his face. He was a thin, dry man packaged in a narrow-lapeled, seersucker suit, somewhat rumpled and a rush on the season. He was watching things with interest. I knew him and knew he was the investigator for the disciplinary committee of the state bar, a tough job. No lawyer makes every client happy. When a client loses it's seldom client's fault, or the lack of evidence, or the possibility that judge and/or jury miscued. It is, of course, his lawyer's fault.

The state man was named Fenwick Tucker. He was here to check me out. He had his big yellow pad and he'd been making copious notes while Sue gave direct evidence. So far, on cross examination, I hadn't impressed him enough to get him started on more notes and I was discouraged a little about that.

Joe Watts, surprisingly, had not yet made his appearance. I'd agreed to begin without him. If special Judge Judson Burke had been irritated by Watts's non-appearance he'd managed to hide it well. Now, while I cross-examined Sue, Judge Burke sat behind his bench in city court, tried to stay awake, and looked now and then longingly at the bright sun outside. He was probably replaying in his mind some difficult holes during the last golf season or planning strategy for the coming season.

I tried hard to remember my own lowered position. Bington had always been a town which enjoys a pecking order. I'd fallen down the line in it. The Senator was dead. What little I'd had going for me had been derived from my deceased partner and from his niche in Bington's hierarchy. No more.

I doubted that Judson Burke gave a damn whether I lived, died, or gave birth to a litter of pups under my counsel table. He was going to give me a fair trial and then a stiff fine and maybe a jail sentence. He might have been all right if the Senator had lived, but the Senator was dead.

"You're positive it was me?" I asked Sue.

"Of course," he said, with assurance in his voice. "I've known you for years, Robak. When you came you were angry at Mr. Watts because you'd lost the bond hearing. You came out to the property demanding to see the scene where your client killed poor Roger Tuttle and you were looking for trouble just like she was." He gave me a prim look. "All three of us who saw you knew it and knew you. And after you hit Mr. Watts then you dared him to do something about it. I guess you'd had too much to drink. You sure smelled like a distillery."

I saw Judge Burke nod knowingly. *Takes one to know one.*

"And I used abusive language?"

He nodded firmly. "Yes. You cursed the three of us and accused Mr. Watts of trying to have his stepdaughter put away so he could rifle her mother's estate. When he informed you to get off the land you wouldn't have it that way." He shook his head. "I told him later he never should have let you come on the place."

"I was pretty brave what with there being three of you and just one of me, wasn't I?"

He shrugged eloquently. He had his story well memorized and I wasn't going to get any variations. He knew I'd gone in my apartment that night and never come back out, probably knew also that the lights had gone out about ten or so, that my neighbors were gone, and that there were no windows I could have slipped out.

He said again: "You'd been drinking."

"When did this happen?"

"Right at eleven o'clock last Thursday night."

"It couldn't have been at ten o'clock, say?"

"Nope. I checked my watch. And I keep it set right. It was eleven o'clock."

"All right," I said. "Just where is Mr. Watts's farm located —how far from Bington?"

"It's about twenty miles up the interstate."

"About a twenty-minute drive from Bington, then?"

He nodded. "That would be about right."

"And, again, you're positive about date and time?"

"Yes I am," he said.

"Did it surprise you when I hit Mr. Watts?"

"We were all surprised," he said, nodding. "None of us thought you'd go that far and cause real trouble. It was a shock." He leaned forward, waiting and watching. Far back in his eyes I saw something. Perhaps it was faint amusement.

I heard some murmuring in the courtroom behind me and turned, although I'd guessed what it was. Judge Steinmetz had arrived. Alvin Suedell watched him, his face without expression except for that place far back in his eyes.

"Once again," I said. "I struck Mr. Watts at his farm nineteen miles from Bington at right around eleven o'clock last Thursday night?"

"Yes. That's right."

"And when you testify about my striking Mr. Watts at that time and place you are telling the plain, unvarnished truth?"

"Certainly."

"Just as you were telling the plain, unvarnished truth in what you testified to at the bond hearing in Judge Steinmetz's court?"

"Right," he said stoutly.

"About the way Roger Tuttle was killed and who killed him?" I asked loudly.

"Yes sir," he answered, just as loudly.

"That's all I have," I said.

Sue gave me a surprised look. He'd been prepared for a hatchet job and I hadn't really done one.

Herman Leaks said: "No re-direct."

Suedell got up from the witness chair and moved out into the courtroom. I saw him nod solemnly at Judge Steinmetz.

Special Judge Judson Burke had also noticed Judge Steinmetz. He roused himself from his dreams of golfing glory to ask: "Is there some way we can help you, Judge Steinmetz?"

Steinmetz shook his bald old head and smiled tolerantly. "Not at the moment, your honor," he rumbled. "I merely have an interest in this case as it involves a member of the local bar." He stretched his legs out and crossed them, smiled winningly at the prosecutor, whom he detested, and frowned at me.

Leaks called Ted Polly.

He was letter perfect on direct examination, an admirable job. By the time he was done once again I was sorry that I'd sleepwalked and laid it on poor Joe Watts that night. I must have done it because they sure had it down pat how I had done it. I guess I've always been a bastard and just not known it. Drunk and mean—that's me.

I got Polly on cross and asked: "You say I hit Mr. Watts without any cause at all?"

"Yes sir, Mr. Robak."

"Were any of you carrying guns?"

He frowned. That was outside instructions, I figured.

"No," he said, taking the best way.

"Do you ever carry a gun, Mr. Polly?"

"No sir. I don't need one." He smiled at me and tensed his muscles a little.

"Do you ever sit on the roof of the Watts house with a rifle?" I asked.

"Sometimes I do."

"Mr. Suedell does too, doesn't he?"

"I don't know. Maybe," he said.

"What are you guarding?"

"Mr. Watts don't like uninvited guests." He grinned at me. "Like you, Mr. Robak."

"And you guard the house for him?"

"I do what he says—what he tells me to do."

I looked inquiringly around the courtroom. Something I'd done had gotten to the man from the disciplinary committee. He was watching me now, sometimes even making squiggles.

"Do you follow people or watch people for him?"

"Not for him, Mr. Robak. But I was worried about you after you come out there. And so I've kind of kept an eye on you since." He nodded.

"I see. Do you know where Mr. Watts is now?"

"I don't know," he said. "He was going to meet us here."

"Tell me again what day and what time it was when I attacked your Mr. Watts."

He smiled patiently at me and went through it again. "Thursday evening, about eleven o'clock."

"After that, on Friday afternoon, didn't you and Mr. Watts try to block my way on a public road near Mr. Watts's place?"

"No sir. We did not."

"You deny then that I had to drive my motor vehicle against Mr. Watts's car in order to get away from you and Mr. Watts?"

"We saw you out snooping around the farm one day, but I don't know what you're talking about—I mean the cars and all. You can ask Mr. Watts or Mr. Suedell."

"I never mentioned Mr. Suedell," I said sharply. "Was he around also?"

He was rattled a little, but well versed. "No. Of course not. There wasn't any incident like you are trying to say."

"Why was I supposed to ask Mr. Suedell about it then?"

Prosecutor Herman Leaks arose indignantly. "I protest this line of questioning, your honor, and object to the last question on the grounds it's irrelevant. Even if what Mr. Robak says happened did happen then it has nothing to do with what we're hearing today."

"I'm done pursuing it with this witness anyway, so the point's moot."

"You're finished with the witness then?" Judge Burke asked crisply. I could see in his eyes he wanted to get this over and head out for a double martini.

"Not yet. I have a few more questions." I went back to my table and rustled my papers a little, while Polly waited.

"What are you building out on that property that you have to guard?"

He was ready for me. "I don't know. I ain't building it. Someone else is. Not Mr. Watts, either."

"Who is?"

He shrugged. "I don't know, but it don't have anything to do with you popping him, does it?"

I gave him a gentle smile. "And here I thought I got to ask the questions."

Judge Burke leaned down, still bored. "Just answer his questions, Mr. Polly."

Polly nodded, unimpressed by all this hocus-pocus. He flexed his great arms. "I don't know what it is," he said.

"All right," I said. "What you've testified to here has been the whole truth, just as your testimony recently in Judge Steinmetz's court about the killing of Roger Tuttle was the whole truth?"

"Yes sir."

"About that construction out there again," I started . . .

Herman Leaks was up again. He hadn't made so many objections in a long time, but he sensed things were his way.

"I'm going to object to any more questions about any

construction on the grounds it's irrelevant to what's being tried here."

"Sustained," Judge Burke said. He looked me over and I couldn't read anything in his cold eyes. "Are you finished with this witness, Mr. Robak?"

"Yes. That's all."

Judson Burke looked down at his watch. For the first time he exhibited a hint of impatience. "And where is your wandering prosecuting witness, Mr. Watts, Herman?"

Leaks shook his head. "I sent the sheriff out to check on him. He was supposed to be here. Mr. Suedell said he had an appointment out of town last night, but would be back and meet them here for the trial."

"We'll give him fifteen more minutes and then I'll have to continue the matter if he hasn't appeared," Burke said.

That didn't sit well with Leaks and it also didn't sit well with me.

"May I call a witness out of order?" I asked courteously.

Judson Burke looked me over carefully. For the first time I read minute interest in his eyes. He smiled at me condescendingly.

"You understand, Mr. Robak, that you need prove nothing?"

"Yes, your honor. I practice law also. I'd like to question Judge Steinmetz and I don't want to keep him waiting. I'm sure he has other and pressing business."

"All right," he said hastily.

Steinmetz came forward and was sworn.

I got him to state his name and we went into his background a bit until I could see that Burke was getting restless.

"Judge Steinmetz, do you know anything about this case being tried today?"

"Not much. I wasn't there as a witness, if that's what you mean."

"And you weren't in my presence at eleven o'clock last Thursday?"

"No I wasn't."

"Where were you at that time on that date?"

"At home," he said and smiled.

Prosecutor Leaks leaned forward, watching me intently. "Were you alone?"

"Yes," he said. "No one else was around."

Leaks relaxed.

"What were you doing?"

"Well it's none of your business, but I'd fixed me a big bourbon and I was drinking it."

Herman Leaks snickered a little.

"Were you engaged in anything else?"

He nodded. "I was talking on the phone."

Now we were at it and suddenly I saw comprehension dawn in Judge Judson Burke's eyes.

"Who were you talking to?"

"Why with you, Mr. Robak," he said.

"Had I called you, Judge?"

"No. I called you."

"And what number did you dial to call me?" I held up my hand to slow his answer. "Did you dial the number at Mr. Watts's place?"

"Of course not. I dialed your home telephone number."

"Do you remember the number?"

"Certainly." He rattled it off.

"How long did we talk?"

"About twenty minutes."

I looked up at Judge Judson Burke. I grinned over at Herman Leaks.

"That's all the questions I have," I said.

In the back of the courtroom Fenwick Tucker, the gentleman from the state bar, got up and closed his notebook with a snap. He gave Steinmetz a wave, smiled vaguely at me, and headed for the door.

Burke beckoned Leaks and me to the bench.

"I'm going to dismiss this pile of crap," Burke said.

Leaks said nothing.

I said: "Thank you, your honor. I was sure the case was safe in your hands."

He looked me over to see if I was being sarcastic, but I kept my face straight.

"Looks like someone might owe you more than just an apology, Robak," Burke said suggestively. The world loves a winner.

"I have some plans," I said coolly. I nodded at Leaks. "You might pass the word to Mr. Watts on that, Mr. Leaks. A big, fat civil suit. Hang his butt end out in the cold rain. It's a shame he didn't come this morning. I'd like to have had him on the witness stand telling about how and what I did to him."

"You got out of it," he said carefully. "That ought to be good enough."

"Tell him it isn't."

"The witnesses made a mistake and got the wrong day is all," he said lamely.

"You prepared the affidavit and took their evidence, Herman. You want to try some other day on for size now? Because that won't work either." I moved toward him. "And how about letting me sign some affidavits against your witnesses for perjury?"

He turned away, saying nothing.

Steinmetz still sat in the witness chair. No one had formally released him.

"Fifty thousand dollars," he said in a loud voice.

We all turned toward him.

"That's the bond for Mary Ann Moffat. I'm going to set it at that figure."

Herman Leaks sputtered darkly. "You can't do that."

Steinmetz smiled. "I just did it, Mr. Leaks. Bond will be fifty thousand dollars." He thought intently for a moment. "I guess maybe that's too high. I'll make it twenty thousand dollars. That's a nice figure."

Leaks shook his head, empires vanishing, face gray.

"The testimony of apparent perjurers isn't enough for a solid case, Mr. Leaks. I now have grave doubts about what happened." He got up out of his chair. "I hereby excuse myself." He nodded at the three of us. "I'll accept such a bond after nine o'clock tomorrow morning, Mr. Robak."

"Thank you," I said.

He marched away regally.

Leaks vanished into the city judge's office where I'm sure they plotted together against me.

I went to the jail and announced the glad tidings to Mary Ann, who kissed me many times.

The funeral was that afternoon. I went to it, again wearing my best suit of the two I own. I suffered through the funeral and then assisted in the loading of the hearse and followed it to the graveyard.

A preacher I vaguely knew once more extolled the Senator's

virtues. The crowd was large. The cemetery was a stone's throw from Abel's Bar, once one of the Senator's favorites. That was good. A watering spot to haunt after hours.

While that was going on, while I was helping with the lifting and lowering of the casket and smelling the final flowers, someone either started a fire in the office or I was in a very bad run of luck.

When I got there after the funeral the fire trucks were spewing water into visible flames inside the office windows. Smoke rose against the April sky. Volunteer firemen rushed here and there. A policeman guarded a rope barrier.

"We thought maybe you was up there," he said to me, without much expression. "If you had been why no one could have gotten you out. It was really a hot one when we first got here."

"I was at the funeral. I saw the smoke and drove up this way."

He nodded. "Bad fire. I guess maybe about everyone in the building was down at the funeral. Whole back end of the building will probably go."

"How'd it start?"

"I don't know," he said. He remembered something. "I think maybe the chief was looking for you."

"All right. Where is he?"

"He's someplace around." He peered through the smoke, but didn't see Handy and finally looked back at the still-burning building. "Sure puts you out of business, doesn't it?" The idea didn't appear to displease him.

I gave him a sour look. I didn't need his affection anyway. I spotted Handy through the acrid smoke and moved toward him.

He was bulwarking the end of the rope line, holding back

the crowd, which had grown since I arrived. I pushed my way roughly toward him. He spotted me and nodded.
"I hope there wasn't anything up there that can't be replaced."
I looked up at the fire red windows where I'd practiced law over some hard years. I shook my head.
"I still got a gun I'd like to give you," he said.
"No. Not my style, Handy. Somebody'd take it away from me and maybe make me eat the front sight off it. Besides, despite a lot of provocation, I don't really want to hurt anyone."
"Then maybe it would be better for you to stay with me for a few days," he said. "I hear they're pretty mad about what went on down at city hall this morning. I carry a gun and I don't suffer from your disability."
I thought about his sterile apartment, the apartment he'd made so lonely. I shook my head. "No, not at your place."
He nodded, understanding. "I'll stay with you then. I got this bad feeling about all this. We both know it isn't done with." He gave me a stubborn look. "When you get your girl out of jail tomorrow then maybe the three of us can move in together for a few days at her place. But I'm not going to leave you by yourself at night. I insist I stay at your place or you stay at mine."
"Okay," I said, giving in. I got out my key chain and took off the apartment key and gave it to him.
He took it and put it in his pocket.
"How'll you get in?"
"There's another key under the mat. I'll use it."
He shook his head in open disgust. "When you do then don't put that key back under the mat. That's the first place

someone wanting to ambush you would look." He stopped and considered me pityingly. "You are a trusting soul."

"Yes, I guess I am."

"That was a cute trick you pulled on them having Judge Steinmetz as a witness. Really broke their backs."

I looked up at the ruined building. In a few short days they'd destroyed or tried to destroy my livelihood, probably killed my partner, perhaps killed Mary Ann's mother, and possibly even done away with drunken Roger Tuttle. No matter what happened to me in the future my life had been dramatically changed. And it seemed very wrong to me that Watts and his friends could change my life without damaging their own.

"Did Watts ever show up around city hall?"

"No. We got some rumors is all. He went someplace last night for an appointment. He didn't tell the others where he was going. I'm guessing he somehow got the word. Maybe someone called Judge Steinmetz. Would he have told someone you were on the phone with him if he'd been asked?"

I hesitated. "He might."

"Watts told the others he'd meet them at court. He owns a place up in the Canadian woods and another in Florida. The sheriff thinks he may have headed for one of those places to stay for a time until he finds out what's going to happen."

"If he found out wouldn't it have been easier just to drop the affidavit against me?"

"Maybe he didn't know for sure," he said.

A uniformed officer came up and tapped him on the back. He turned away.

"I'll see you later," I said.

He nodded abstractedly, trying to concentrate on what the officer was telling him. He gave me a little wave.

Everything seemed to me as if it was moving too fast. I left the Plymouth where it was, left the avid crowd to *oooh* and *ahhh* about the last of the fire, and walked on down to the Moose Club. I used my dues card to gain entrance and went in, ordered an Early Times from a remote bartender and carried it to an empty booth in the darkest corner.

I sat down and put my feet up on the rung of the booth. I went over it in my head again, but there was no light, no light at all.

Someone had scratched graffiti into the table of my booth. The most readable slogan was: *Slow down stupid*. It seemed on the subject.

Two amiable drunks argued baseball at the bar. In my present frame of mind I wasn't sure they wouldn't draw guns on each other to settle their argument.

After a while I ordered a sandwich and ate it silently, not wanting to talk with anyone, although several people I knew came in.

There was a moth fluttering in my head. To still it I went to a pay phone in the lobby and dialed Virginia's number.

She answered after a few rings.

"This is Don, Virginia. I need to know something."

"Go to hell," she said softly, but she didn't hang up.

"I probably will. Before I start, was the Senator involved in some sort of condemnation action I didn't know about? Something going on now?"

"No he wasn't."

"Positive?"

"Very positive."

"Thank you," I said.

"I'm giving notice, Mr. Robak."

"All right, Virginia."

"I apologize for telling you to go to hell," she said, but I didn't think she meant it.

I hung the phone up gently and walked from the Moose up to where I'd parked the Plymouth. The night air cleared my head fog.

The office building was roped off. The whole back end of the building had fallen in. There would be nothing to salvage there.

I drove to my apartment and let myself in with the rug key, dutifully pocketing same after I'd unlocked the door.

The apartment was silent. I turned on the television and watched an old Humphrey Bogart movie, still thinking.

I was at the edge of sleep when Handy came in. He clucked at me and went around pulling drapes tight shut after making sure the windows were locked.

"Your neighbors still gone?"

"Yes. Thanks for coming past, but I'm a big boy now and you don't have to do this."

He smiled. "I don't have many friends. I can't stand losing even one of them." He looked away from me and maybe he was remembering another time and place.

I kept drifting off. Handy made coffee, but I just got sleepier. I was worn out, but I fought sleep.

There was a reason. A cold and chilling reason.

But I went to bed.

Once, sometime later, I almost came up from sleep because the phone rang and I felt I had to answer.

But I went back to sleep. I couldn't stay awake. I dreamed. In the dream everything was unfocused, but still I could see things and they were frightening things. There was darkness and sound and stinging pain in my arm. All fantasy. All unsure.

And . . . Then . . . There . . .
Nothingness. A lack.

———◆———

When I awoke I was confused. There was an absence of light, but I wasn't in my bed. My first thought was that Handy had to be dead back there in my apartment, growing cold now. I wondered how they'd done it.

My head hurt a lot.

I tried to reason about what was going on. I could tell I was sitting somewhere on a seat that gave a little as I squirmed about on it. My feet and legs, below the knees, were trussed up to my chest so that I was in a fetal position. There was no feeling of solidity anywhere except under me and in my right arm. That arm was tied to something. There were many loops around it made of some kind of smooth and elastic tape. I could move it a little, even extend it some. My left arm was bound tight against my body, but my left hand was free. I pushed my left arm against whatever held it and there was a little give there, but not much.

My eyes were covered. The darkness was very frightening. I wanted to call out. I could do that. There was no tape or gag over my mouth. It seemed, therefore, a foolish thing to do, but I began doing it anyway. Surely whoever had carefully tied and trussed me wasn't going to let me yell my way out of it. If screaming would be a help to me then I thought I'd be wearing multiple gags. Nothing happened when I yelled.

I moved a bit more against the seat under me and it gave and squeaked with my movement and there was something familiar about it, as if I'd known it before. I drew in a breath of air, sniffing it, and the smell was familiar also. I moved some more, making springs squeak again and feeling the tiny sting of a sharp end through padding.

I knew where I was.

I was tied up in my own car, unable to move. My stomach churned and I felt clammy and sick.

Mary Ann's mother might have felt about the same way if she'd been conscious in the moments before she died. I shivered and fought briefly with my fastenings, but they were secure, put there by an expert or experts and there seemed no hope about them. I went back to considering other things, trying hard to fight down panic.

In a little while, as I sat there, I heard footsteps and the sound stiffened my spine a little. The car shifted weight so that I leaned in the direction of the downward shift as the driver's door opened. Someone got in beside me.

I said: "Take the blindfold off."

All movement beside me stopped as my request was considered.

"I know who you are," I said.

No reaction from beside me.

"I want to see what's going to happen."

Again, nothing.

I jerked hard against the bonds, trying to get my right arm high enough and my head low enough to erase the blindfold, but all was secure and I was a foot short.

I relapsed into silence, waiting for him/her to say something. Somewhere, far away, I heard the sound of a heavy motor, accelerating, changing gears. It seemed far away, maybe miles.

I said to the silence: "I mailed a letter last night before I went home. I sent copies of it to lots of people. No one's going to believe this. I wrote down what's happened and why. And I made some phone calls from the Moose Club."

Still nothing.

And so I said the name.
Suddenly, right then, I knew the name. Now that I had to have it it was mine.

I heard him suck in his breath quickly and he laughed just a little. There was the feeling of rough hands at the back of my head and, suddenly, the blindfold was gone. The bright penny April sun shone through the car windows, blinding me for a moment. I blinked my eyes for focus and only half opened them.

We were on a country lane, a path of a road I'd never seen before. It was somewhere near the interstate because, through the trees, I could see a small stretch of that road in the far distance.

"Thank you," I said. I'd read stories about people who died by the ax and in the hundreds of other interesting ways we figure for each other. Some of those stories had been about relationships that began between headsman and victim, so that there was almost an affection between them. I felt that way now.

He smiled at me gently. "I'm sorry," he said. "There aren't any letters, though. And I won't worry about your phone calls. Too bad you have to die."

I nodded, not caring yet, still grateful at being out of the darkness. I inspected myself. I was tied up like a rib roast. My left arm had been strapped to my side, so that only my hand and its fingers were easily movable. Similar straps, of the kind you sometimes see restraining mental patients, held my legs up against my chest. My right arm was tied to the right post of the car door. I rested uncomfortably in that position on the seat of my Plymouth.

He watched me with cold eyes. "Makes a good launching pad. When I come to an emergency stop the rope will act as a guide for you into the windshield and the front door and windshield post. Sometimes I have to do it more than once. I'd hoped you wouldn't wake up, but there are benefits both ways. This way I can ask you some things. But it will be easier for both of us after you're unconscious and out of it. Then, when you're dead, I'll remove your bindings. I'll walk out to my own car after wrecking yours. My car isn't far away. I'll leave you for someone else to find." He smiled at me. "It will be quick for you."

"How nice of you," I said. "But it won't wash. If I hit the door post on the driver's side, your side, then that's normal, but the one on the right side isn't normal. Someone will notice." I nodded confidently, but it was a forlorn hope.

He shook his head, still smiling. "Thousands die in auto accidents every year. No one gets upset about vehicle deaths. Your friends will shake their heads and slow their speeds for a day or two and then you'll be forgotten. They'll think you were upset at the death of the Senator and weren't watching what you were doing. They'll talk about how this old clunker of an auto finally got you. No one will think anything other than just an accident." He inspected his hands. "I know. I've done this before."

"You mean Mrs. Watts?"

He nodded. "And a few before her." He shook his head, remembering. "It's a thing I dreamed up. All I really need to do is get your car up to say sixty or seventy miles an hour. Then I hit the brakes—hard—a panic stop. The car abruptly slows, but you, unheld by a seat belt or your legs, don't stop. You continue on forward at the same speed the car had at the time of my braking. You can't stop yourself. You smash into the windshield and the door frame. I've got you strapped so that your right arm will guide you there. I do it until you're dead. You'll probably make it through the first time. Some do. But eventually you'll die. Then I'll take your car to a spot I've picked out close and run it off the road and into a tree."

"You had Mrs. Watts tied up like this," I said. "That's what dislocated and fractured her arm."

"Yes," he said.

I measured things with my own eyes mathematically and concluded he was right about what would happen.

He looked away from me and said: "I'm sorry about the Senator. He started making calls and rocking the boat. Watts didn't like it. There was just too much at stake to let him go on. He got angry and tried to run away and he fell. He just stayed down on the floor and began to breathe funny and turned dark and died. So I didn't have to do anything. And I only need a few days more. They paid us half the cash down and the other half is next week. Watts took the stock, but I get the cash—or most of it."

"How much?" I asked.

"So much you'd never believe it. They got a bought deal going on over in their state on a jetport. I don't even know how it works and don't much care. That was Joe Watts's part. We had to make it look like we were subdividing the land. You're a lawyer. Lots are more valuable than raw land. So the building corporation will sell out to the jetport authority for a lot of money."

I remembered the condemnation cases. The Senator had begun to do some figuring.

"Did you kill a man named Rossi for Watts?"

"Who?" he asked uncomprehendingly.

"He was the man who was the tenant on the first farm Watts bought out there."

"I remember the name now. He died accidentally, I guess."

"Where's Watts?" I asked.

He shook his head, not hearing me, counting the money over and over in his mind.

He said: "The agreement is that they pay the money end off in cash and bearer bonds. It's money out of an old political fund that they're afraid to even give back now. I don't know about the way the stock was supposed to split up or who was involved." He shook his head. "Everyone thought Watts had so much, but he was almost broke—at least for him he was broke. This had to work out or he thought he was finished. Then people kept getting in the way."

"Where is Watts?" I asked again.

"I hear it might be Canada," he said. "Or maybe Mexico." He gave me another smile. It couldn't hurt to tell me and he wanted to tell someone. "But no one will ever find him if they look in those places." He looked away from me, remembering. "You know upstream above Riversburg about a mile there's a place below a bluff where the river's a hundred feet deep a few feet out from shore."

"Why?" I asked.

"He had to keep rocking the boat. He gave that woman her contract and promised her a part of the money that was to be mine. Then he chased that Mary Ann doll and made her mother angry enough so that she started rattling the contract and he had to promise her even more to hold her still. Then, when I take care of her, damned if he doesn't let that drunken Roger Tuttle see all the money and so they had to kill him. If it had been me I'd have given him a few thousand bucks and enough booze to drink himself to death."

"Mary Ann didn't kill Tuttle?" I asked.

"No, but you'd never been able to prove it. It happened about like they said in court. She took her shot and didn't hit anything. The three of them were taking Tuttle out to the electric fence. They were going to push him into it and see what happened. So she was a gift. The gun went off in the struggle, but no one was hurt. They reloaded a chamber and shot him with her gun after she was out of it." He looked at me inquiringly. "Did she have the contract on her person then?"

"In her purse," I said. "But she doesn't have it any more."

"That's what they were looking for both times in your office, you know. I didn't have anything to do with it."

I nodded.

"Where is it?" he asked.

"It burned up in the office," I lied.

"Maybe. Maybe not." He thought for a minute. "Where was it before she gave it to you?"

"In her purse. A deputy let her take her purse into the jail. It's against the rules, but she's an attractive girl and so he bent the rules."

"We checked there."

"No one ever tells about breaking a rule," I said. "Did you check her cell?"

"No." He looked away from me. "Watts held some of the money back from me. He was a man who thought he was number one. I still don't know where that money is that he held, but I'll collect the second installment—all of it. I don't think he really believed I was going to drop him in the river until I let him fall. I hung a car bumper on his feet. But he worried me. He got you and the Senator interested in Mary Ann and he kept the feud hot when it should have been cool. Sue and Polly don't even know about me. They know there was someone, but they don't know it was me. Watts would call me when he needed something." He stopped and considered things again, making sure within himself that he was right. "I got him to make me the bag man. I convinced him it was safer that way. Then he held part of the money I was supposed to get away from me. Now the boys in the next state will pay the rest to me. It's all done, but the wait. Watts wasn't necessary any more. A liability. He wanted to be God."

"Someone will find him," I said. "They'll never stop looking. He was a big man."

"Not for a long time. With that bumper tied to him he won't float for a long time. Maybe never. Lots of bodies in that river that float up just are never identified."

"You can't kill this many people in a small town and not make trouble. Mary Ann's mother, Tuttle, Watts, and now me," I said.

"Who's killed? You and Mrs. Watts died in auto accidents, the Senator had a heart attack, and Watts ran off after he failed to appear against you in a trial he tried to rig. Two years from now they'll be constructing their jetport up there on his farm and all of you dead ones will be forgotten."

"Why'd Watts want the contract?"

"He talked to some lawyer who said he ought to get it. He was afraid that it might mess up the land deal."

"She signed the deeds," I said.

He shrugged. "The lawyer still thought it would be a good idea for Watts to collect all the copies of the contract."

"I figured it was you. Someone else will."

He looked out the car window. Tiny lines appeared near his eyes. "That's the real reason why I took the blindfold off—the best reason anyway. The contract can't hurt me, but I wanted to know how you knew it was me." He gave me a suspicious look. "Could you see out of that blindfold?"

"No. It was tight. But there were a lot of things."

He looked down the tiny road and examined his watch. "There's some time left. Tell me."

"What are we waiting for?" I temporized.

He pointed out the window. "At the end of this lane there's a county road. There are only a few families that live back it now. The county road used to go through to Paintstown, but the bridge washed out this last winter. Maybe it's the most deserted place in the whole county. I found it a few months back and sort of tucked it in the back of my mind for when I'd need it." His voice was easy, conversational. "Only time you can expect a vehicle on the road is about five minutes from now when a school bus comes in and turns around on the other side of this lane. No one gets out. I guess this is just the place where the driver's always turned. So we wait until he's past. After that there may not be anyone along for hours. It's a good chance. And it's right north of the estate that Watts once owned. A logical place for you to be found." He looked out the front window again, waiting for the bus. "Now, tell me how you knew."

"Okay, Handy," I said. I looked into his cloudless blue eyes and we smiled at each other.

"One more thing," I said, before starting. "I figured that the guarding of the Watts property wasn't guarding of the property at all, but of what was inside. But why did you keep trying to give me a gun?"

"I thought maybe you might try to get in out there. They were waiting for you." He looked away and then back, grinning. "And the gun has a defective firing pin. It don't shoot."

I nodded.

"You didn't know last night it was me," he said.

"Things were happening too quickly for me to sort them, but I was about finished working it out last night."

"A little late."

"Yes," I said. "I guess it was. But you made some mistakes. They'll be enough to catch you eventually, Handy. You're so in love with vehicular death and how easy it is that you were sloppy on the Watts woman's 'accident.' No real frame damage. Maybe you took a hammer and maybe an ax to the Fibreglas body to make things look better, but you were lazy about it." I looked at him. "Are you going to take a hammer to my Plymouth?"

He nodded. "If I can't make it look realistic enough without one."

"The tree you used on Mrs. Watts was cut off too high for chance, although it didn't mean a thing by itself. Then Watts got shook up and smacked little Sydney Clark around when he talked about how those Corvettes can be shredded. A guilty conscience in advance." I looked at him again. "But do you know what really clinched it for me?"

He waited.

"Your accident report that you so painstakingly made out showed skid marks longer than the distance from Watts's gate to the tree stump. I figure it was a slip you made because you knew the car had traveled down the asphalt road, driven by you of course, and not out of the gate."

"I put that on the accident report?" he asked unbelievingly.

"You did."

He raised his eyes to heaven.

"It had to be you, Handy."

"Why not Watts?"

"He'd have shown up yesterday morning. He hated me because of Mary Ann and he thought he had me good. When he didn't appear I figured he had to be incapacitated or dead. If Steinmetz had told him I had an alibi he'd not have let Polly and Sue come."

"All right," he said. "Then Sue and Polly?"

"Not Polly for sure. I've known him for a lot of years. He's a small-timer, strong, but unbright, not very swift upstairs. And Sue was always the one I saw on the roof. Someone had to tell him to do that. Otherwise he'd have been playing cards."

"There's your good friend Herman Leaks, the prosecutor? A passion killing? He was after Mrs. Watts once."

I nodded. "I'm still not sure that Watts didn't put Herman up to romancing Mrs. Watts to try to bring things to a head and help get rid of her. If she'd been the only one who died I might have bought that. But too many people died, people that Herman didn't have anything to do with. And Herman already has what he wants—a gal with money to finance his future in politics—if he has any future."

"There was a lot of money around in this. I imagine that Watts let some of it rub off on Herman."

"Still comes up you, Handy. You used to work for Watts in Detroit. I'll bet you five against one that you figured this out in theory when you were some kind of test driver up there."

"Good guess." He looked at me and something changed in his eyes, so that they lost their calm look. "I never could get Watts to admit he was the one called it on my wife."

"But that's why you killed him, and not the money," I said softly.

He nodded almost imperceptibly and went on: "Not even when I had him up on the cliff. I got a couple of people in Detroit. That was a good place to learn the advantages of a quiet car wreck." He gave me a look in which there was still frustration. "I never could actually get it back to Watts. No one knew who'd ordered it. My guess is it was done by telephone, then the money mailed." He shook his head, not sure. "But I was sure."

"Mary Ann overheard it was 'the driver.'"

"How's that?"

"Watts talked some in his sleep the night of Mrs. Watts's funeral. His talking made her move out of the house and was also the reason why she took a shot at him."

"He wanted her out anyways," he said. "The money was there."

"If there was all that money why didn't he just pay off Mrs. Watts?"

"She wanted the full amount. And she knew where the money was coming from. So he called me."

"What now?" I asked.

"There's all the money, Don. I'd like to have you with me to help spend it, but that would never work out. I guess I'll buy me a piece of an island someplace." He moved restlessly, not sure of himself again. "I'll have a lot of women and a lot of good times. I'll forget Detroit, forget Bington."

"Sure," I said.

He started the car. Down below, but far away, I could see the yellow school bus gleaming in the sun. Was there a way to attract their attention?

"Forget it," he said. "He's made his turn. It won't be long for you now," he said over the sound of the motor.

I looked around and I saw one thing that came in clearly to me. I saw the seat belt he'd hooked around his waist. It was a little too far, but maybe I could stretch it. I'd have to.

If I launched off the passenger seat door, stretched everything, and timed it just right, I might get it done.

A chance.

I pulled my body farther from his with my tied right arm and got myself back into the corner of the front seat.

The school bus vanished down the road and still he waited. He turned to me and smiled once more, not angry at me, maybe even sorry. It wasn't the way I wanted him. I wanted him angry.

He started down the road. We left the lane and he stepped down on the accelerator.

He said: "I'm sorry, Don. I really am."

"No you're not," I said, letting the hate come out, thinking how it could be done. We were picking up speed.

"You were never sorry. Not in your whole life. Not even when your wife and child died."

His face went stony and he pushed the accelerator of the Plymouth down as hard as he could and we bucked and jolted down the road. I could see the speedometer out of the corner of my eye, but I watched his right foot. The time would be when he raised it to stamp down on the brake.

A rabbit darted across the road in front of us and he cursed and I almost launched myself, but held back in time.

Sixty miles an hour on gravel is like a hundred on asphalt. The springs in the Plymouth squealed in protest and the old motor hammered itself toward extinction.

He looked over at me in the corner with his damaged restless stare and lifted his foot and I launched, pushing off as hard as I could. I felt my left hand brush across the belt and nothing seemed to happen for a millisecond and it all seemed lost. Then the seat belt flipped away and he came forward, bracing himself with his foot on the brake and his hands clenched to the wheel, not really in danger yet. I was sliding, but when he came forward my left hand caught at him and held to his coat as he slid toward me. My hand pulled him even farther as I fought the force of the stop.

His foot slipped away from the brake and he lost control of the car. It skidded in the slick gravel to the right and then to the left. He was still coming over my way and the skids threw me a little toward him and behind him, so that now he was to the front, his body partially cushioning mine. *Milliseconds, milliseconds.*

The Plymouth went sideways and rolled. I was knocked here and there, and there was pain and hurt and fright. The car began to rock more gently and then motion stopped. Handy was all the way in front of me. He didn't move, but his eyes were open and in focus. I felt pain in a number of places. My right arm felt as if it had been torn away, but I saw it hadn't, although it was at a curious angle.

Blood was on me, but most of it didn't seem to be mine. I could see that Handy was bleeding very copiously from a deep cut in his neck.

He said weakly: "My neck. If you can move off me maybe I can get my hands up there and stop the bleeding."

I nodded, but I didn't try very hard. If he could stop the bleeding then maybe he could start some of mine. Besides my right arm wouldn't work at all and I couldn't seem to find the energy to push myself away from him.

In a little while his bleeding slowed and finally it stopped. His eyes never closed, but he stopped breathing.

I blacked out a long, hideous time later.

When I awoke I had a lot of equipment around me. I could see bright sun outside.

And Mary Ann at the side of the bed.